MW01254799

Murder Under A Black Moon

A Mona Moon Mystery
Book Six

Abigail Keam

Worker Bee Press

ISBN 978 1 7329743 9 5
09 21 2020

Published in the USA by

Worker Bee Press
P.O. Box 485
Nicholasville, KY 40340

1

Mona entered the Moon box at Churchill Downs in order to watch the Kentucky Derby.

"Is she here—somewhere?" Aunt Melanie stammered, craning her neck around Mona. Before Mona could take her seat, Melanie pushed her aside to get a better look at the people milling behind them.

Flabbergasted, Mona hurriedly took a seat. "For goodness sake, Melanie. Get a hold of yourself. Mrs. Longworth is with Lord Farley checking the horses out in the paddock."

"I'm going to greet her."

Mona grabbed Melanie's arm. "Sit down, please. She'll be here shortly. Then you can talk her arm off."

"How did you manage to wrangle Alice Roosevelt Longworth as a house guest?"

"I didn't. Lord Farley is her host. Apparently, the Roosevelts and Farleys are related. She wanted to come to the Derby and called Lord Farley up."

Melanie looked crestfallen. "You mean she's not staying at Moon Manor?"

"Afraid not. She's Lord Farley's guest."

"Quit referring to Robert as Lord Farley. We all know he is Lawrence Robert Emerton Dagobert Farley, Marquess of Gower," Melanie snapped. "And we all know you two are engaged. Stop rubbing it in."

Mona grinned. "It's eating you up, isn't it, Aunt Melanie?"

"You know it is. I had my cap set on Robert. Then my brother had the rude manners to make you his sole heir to the Moon fortune, and up and died on me before I could get the will changed. Without you butting in, I'm sure Robert would have fallen for me." Melanie straightened her hat. "I can't wait to see Manfred and give him a piece of my mind."

Mona studied her aunt to see if Melanie recognized the irony of her statement. Melanie would have to be dead in order to talk with her brother. It was a shame Melanie never saw the futility of her life. She was a lovely-looking woman with light eyes and blonde hair with pale ivory skin. She and Mona looked very much alike, but Mona's hair was platinum and her eyes a startling yellow—only two percent of the world's population had eyes the color of Mona's. They were near the same age as Melanie was the last bloom of her mother's womb. When Melanie was very small, Mona's father (Melanie's brother) married against his parent's wishes and left Moon Manor disinherited. But that's where the sameness ended as their temperaments were worlds apart.

Mona was a hard worker and college-educated, whereas Melanie whiled away her days lunching and gossiping with the "girls." Her education had been a Swiss finishing school that molded young women into potential helpmates for powerful men.

"You know that Alice and FDR aren't speaking because she supported Herbert Hoover running for president instead of her own cousin."

"Is that so?" Mona replied.

Melanie sniffed, "It's not the first public quarrel she's had. She supposedly buried a voodoo doll of William Howard Taft's daughter, Nellie, in the White House lawn after Taft won the presidency. Both the Taft and Wilson administrations banned her from the White House. I guess it will be only a matter of time before she does likewise with this administration."

"Bury an effigy of Mrs. Roosevelt in the White House lawn?" Mona teased.

"Ugh, Eleanor. I can't stand that high-pitched voice of hers—like nails squeaking on a chalkboard. Well, yes, I mean that Alice will do something that will get her banned from the White House again."

"And yet she is so popular."

"You know her father, Teddy Roosevelt—"

"I know who her father was, Melanie," Mona cut in.

Melanie continued unabashed, "Her father, President Theodore Roosevelt, said, 'I can be President of the United States, or I can control Alice. I cannot possibly do both.'"

Mona looked over her shoulder. Robert and Alice had been gone for a long time. She wondered what was holding them up. "Look at the crowd. Half the people are here to see the Derby and the other half to see Alice Roosevelt. I wonder who tipped the papers that she was coming."

"I have no idea," Melanie said nonchalantly, looking through her binoculars at the crowd.

Mona gave Melanie a hard look as she was suspicious of her aunt. Very few people knew Alice Roosevelt Longworth was coming, but there was always the possibility Miss Alice could have tipped off the papers herself.

Melanie leaned over and nudged Mona. "You know it is rumored Alice Roosevelt's daughter is not her husband's but sired by Senator William Borah."

"Who was sired by Senator Borah?" Willie Deatherage asked, entering the Moon private viewing box with a small tray of Mint Julep drinks and handed one to Mona and Melanie.

"Thank you, dear," Mona said. "Very thoughtful of you."

Melanie said, "I so love this drink. Wouldn't be Derby Day without a Mint Julep." Seeing Willie's stricken face, Melanie added, "Oh, sorry,

Willie. I forgot that you are on the wagon."

Willie took her seat and ignored Melanie's snide remark. She made it a habit long ago to pay little attention to the woman.

Dexter Deatherage, his hands full of drinks also, stumbled into the box. "Here, someone help me before I drop these. I got extras because I don't want to be running up and down the aisles for refreshments."

Mona and Willie reached over and relieved Dexter of his burden.

"Who are we talking about now?" Dexter asked, handing his wife a cold Coca Cola bottle from his pocket and a ginger ale from his other pocket.

"I was saying that it is rumored that Paulina Longworth is not the child of Nicholas Long-worth, but Senator William Borah," Melanie said.

"This is unseemly talk," Mona admonished. "Gossip like this can ruin a woman."

Ignoring Mona, Willie said, "I heard she wanted to name the baby Deborah. Get it—de Borah. The family nicknamed the child Aurora Borah Alice."

Dexter suggested, "Ladies, quit talking about

our distinguished guest like that. It is scandalous."

"Oh, Dexter, you're such a stick-in-the-mud," Willie complained about her husband.

"Be that as it may, my dearest, let's show some decorum. Robert and Alice will be here any moment. I passed them on the way."

Mona asked, "What's taking them so long?"

"Mrs. Longworth is being bombarded by the crowds wanting her autograph or presenting her with Teddy bears. They're making their way through slowly."

"Aren't the Pinkertons keeping the crowds away?" Mona asked, perturbed. The last thing she wanted was for Alice Roosevelt Longworth, daughter of a popular dead U.S. President to be harmed on her watch.

Dexter answered, "It seems Mrs. Longworth is having a grand time meeting her devoted public. The Pinkertons are helpless but to obey her commands."

Mona sighed in relief until she heard sharp voices rise from the spectator box next to theirs as a young man and woman were arguing. "Melanie, let me see those binoculars."

Melanie swung the binoculars over to the couple.

"What are they saying?" Willie asked.

"They are arguing over another woman," Melanie said.

An older couple tried to quiet them down. Finally, the young woman burst into tears and rushed out of the box. The middle-aged couple and the young man looked astonished. The young man started to rush after the fleeing woman, but the older woman pulled him back and coaxed him into his seat.

Mona assumed the older couple were the young man's parents. Grabbing the binoculars from Melanie, she said, "Give back my binoculars. I wish you'd buy your own."

"I would if you upped my pitiful stipend."

"Oh, stop with that. You make more money in a year than ninety-nine percent of the country."

"You can never be too rich or too thin," Melanie replied.

"Who are they?" Mona asked.

Melanie scrunched her nose and said, "They are Jeannie and Zeke Duff. New money. Oil wells from somewhere west of the Pecos I expect. The young chap in the seersucker suit is their son Cody."

Willie shot Melanie a disdainful look. "They are oil people from Texas. They had black gold on their land and cashed in. They have relocated here and are itching to break into the horse business."

"Good luck to them," Melanie said, ruefully. "They are nothing but social climbers as far as I'm concerned. The last thing the Bluegrass needs is more parvenus."

Willie rolled her eyes.

"And the young woman?" Mona asked.

Willie added, "The tearful woman is his new bride, Helen."

Dexter added, "From Texas as well."

Willie said, "I hear they are having a difficult time blending in, especially the new wife. She wants to go back to Texas."

"I can attest to how difficult it is to make friends here if one is new," Mona said.

"I resent that," Willie teased.

"I don't mean you and Dexter, of course, but born and bred Lexingtonians are very snobbish.

You must admit that, Willie."

"We don't like to see new money come in and buy up our land," Willie said.

Dexter argued, "But, darling, the old aristocrats don't have the money to hang on to these farms. They are expensive to run. The Depression has hit everyone. Look at John Keene. He wants to sell his farm for Lexington's new racecourse, and his family has been here since the 1700s."

"Well, the Wrights didn't do so badly buying land for Calumet Farm," Melanie concurred. "Old man Wright saved the land from the bulldozer."

Willie mused, "I wonder how it's going with the son changing it from a Standardbred horse farm to a Thoroughbred horse farm. Big difference in training."

"I saw Warren Wright the other day. He said things were going fine at Calumet Farm, and he hopes to have a champion soon," Mona said.

"Don't hold your breath," Melanie scoffed. "He's got nothing but plugs at the moment."

"I'm not sure I would agree, Melanie," Dexter said. "Warren Wright is a sharp cookie."

Melanie harrumphed.

"Who are the other couples in their box?" Willie asked.

Melanie strained her neck in order to get a good gander. "The woman in the red dress and big Derby hat is Natasha Merriweather and her husband Tosh. She is the daughter of an iron magnate and, like the Duffs, wants to learn the racing business. They recently bought Pennygate Farm."

Mona nodded. "I had heard Pennygate had been sold."

"Well, they bought it," Willie added.

"And the other couple?" Mona asked.

Melanie stood and twisted toward their neighboring box, waving to some friends who had yoo-hooed her. Sitting back down, she said, "That's Rusty Thompson and his wife. He's a trainer and buyer for folks who have cash to burn."

"Was," Dexter said.

Mona turned to watch Dexter take a sip of his Mint Julep. "What do you mean by 'was?'"

Willie fanned herself with a racing program. "Mona, don't you know anything that's going on in town?"

Mona laughed, "I've been preoccupied."

"Did you say you've been preoccupied, darling? I hope it's because you've been planning our wedding."

Mona looked up and smiled. There Robert was—the light of her life.

Robert escorted a distinguished looking woman wearing a blue chiffon day dress into the Moon spectator box. "Everyone, I'd like you to meet my guest, Mrs. Nicholas Longworth."

Everyone in the box stood in greeting as did everyone around them who was eavesdropping.

Mrs. Longworth took her program and patted Robert on the chest with it. "Dear boy, always introduce a woman by her own name. I hate that ancient practice of introducing a woman by her husband's name, especially if he's deceased. Rather Edwardian, don't you think?"

Grinning, Robert gave a small bow. "Excusez-moi, Madame. May I present Alice Roosevelt Longworth."

"I found the name of Alice Roosevelt gets me in the better addresses rather than Longworth, and I only refer to my dead husband's name when I need money from the bank."

Everyone twittered.

Mona felt Willie give her a small nudge as if to say "I told you so."

Robert helped Alice to her seat and took the one next to her before introducing everyone.

Alice gave the once-over to Melanie and Mona. "You girls sure stick out with your hair color. Are you sisters?"

"I am Melanie Moon, Miss Alice."

"I got that in the introduction."

"Mona is my niece."

Alice gave Mona a long hard stare. "So, you are the cartographer who runs Moon Enterprises. Everyone is losing their shirts, but Moon Enterprises is having a profitable year and employing more men. My hat off to you, young woman."

"Thank you, Miss Alice. High praise coming from you."

"I think of such people as yourself as the real key to getting this country back on its feet rather than my cousin's ridiculous federal programs. People need to rely on themselves and not the government to get them out of a jam."

"I find that people who hold such beliefs are people with lots of money at their disposal," Mona countered.

Willie murmured, "Oh boy, here we go." She gulped down some ginger ale, knowing of Mona's strong support for FDR's New Deal programs and Alice's dislike of them.

Melanie interjected, "I think what my niece means is—"

Alice cut in, "I know exactly what your niece means. You interested in politics, Miss Moon?"

"Not really, but I help those less fortunate where I can, but call me Mona, please."

"I shall."

Mona leaned forward. "You and I agree on this, Miss Alice—it's jobs that are going to turn this country around. Putting men back to work. The unemployment rate is still twenty-one percent."

Alice asked, "You interested in politics, Melanie?"

Melanie scoffed, "Hardly."

"I'm surprised."

"Why is that?"

"Because politics is a blood sport, and I think you might be pretty good at blood sports."

"Thank you, Miss Alice," Melanie replied in a small voice. She wasn't sure if she had just been insulted or praised.

"Enough of this bantering," Robert said. "The race is getting ready to start."

Everyone stood to sing the Kentucky Derby anthem—My Old Kentucky Home. After the song, there was a crowd murmur as the Derby horses pranced onto the racetrack. Once all horses were placed in the starting gate, a bell rang and they were off with the crowd rushing onto the track itself and running behind the horses.

AND THEY'RE OFF! Peace Chance and Mata Hari speed off with Mata Hari stepping into the lead. Turning in front of the stand with the mob screaming loudly, Mata Hari is in the lead at three comfortable lengths with Quasimodo second and Speedmore third. On the backstretch, it's Mata Hari opening up with Sgt. Byrne now head to head. At the mile post, it's Sgt. Byrne now in front with Mata Hari second. Cavalcade now coming up and challenging both Sgt. Bryne and Mata Hari. Heading home, it's Cavalcade on the outside with Discovery shooting ahead. Cavalcade and Discovery fighting it out as Mata Hari and Sgt. Byrne fade. Two hundred yards to go, it's Discovery in front and here comes Cavalcade fighting for the roses. They are neck to neck with Cavalcade not giving up. Cavalcade is too much for Discovery. Cavalcade can't be stopped, and it's Cavalcade two and a half lengths ahead. Cavalcade wins the sixtieth run of the Kentucky Derby! Discovery is second and Agrarian comes in third!

Robert tore up his ticket. "That does it. I bet on Mata Hari. She just gave out."

"I told you to bet on Cavalcade. Look at his wide chest. Lungs are what wins these races," Alice said, looking smug and holding up her ticket. "I'm going to cash mine in."

A piercing scream rang out over the noise of the crowd, causing everyone to search for the source.

Mona stood. "I don't think that scream sounded like someone who has the winning ticket."

"Or they lost the winning ticket," Willie said.

The scream sounded again and continued into a low mournful hum. Another woman started screaming and sobbing.

"It's coming from the next box!" Mona said.

Everyone in the next box was huddled around a man slumped over in his seat.

"What happened? Do you need help?" Dexter called out as he climbed over the rail that divided the review boxes.

Mona and Robert followed Dexter into the next box.

"Do you need a doctor?" Mona asked a pale and sweating Zeke Duff.

Duff replied, "No, I'm afraid we need the police!" He pointed to the man slumped over.

Mona went over to feel for a pulse when Dexter grabbed her hand. "Don't touch him, Mona. He is beyond your ministrations."

Mona looked closer and noticed small drops of blood trickling down the man's shirt and tie. It was then she realized the unfortunate man was truly dead and caught the sight of the gruesome cause.

The victim had a woman's hat pin protruding from his bloodied left eye!

2

Detective McCaw wetted his pencil with his tongue before writing in his pocket notebook. "What's your name?"

"Madeline Mona Moon."

"The reason you are here?"

"The same reason the other sixty thousand people are—to watch the Kentucky Derby."

"Who are you with?"

"This is a family box—the Moon family box."

Detective McCaw looked up from his notes at Mona. "You mean that Moon family?"

"Yes."

Detective McCaw didn't seem impressed, which caused Mona to take a liking to him. The detective was a rugged-looking man with a ruddy complexion and close-cropped hair. He smelled of Aqua Velva shaving lotion, and a thick scar ran from his left ear down his neck. His clothes were pressed and clean, but his shoes were grimy. Mona deduced he must have been working on another murder prior to this one, which had occurred in a muddy field. One of Detective McCaw's eyelids twitched a bit. Mona wondered if that was a remnant of the trauma that had to do with the scar. McCaw was not handsome, but wonderfully masculine—the kind of man who naturally draws women to him.

"What's your address?"

"Mooncrest Farm, Lexington, Kentucky."

"Who is in your party?"

"My lawyer, Dexter Deatherage, and his wife, Wilhelmina. Robert Farley, my fiancé. My aunt, Melanie Moon, and Mrs. Alice Longworth."

"Is this Alice Longworth related to you as well?"

Mona gave Detective McCaw a blank look. "You're pulling my leg, of course." She couldn't believe McCaw didn't recognize one of the most famous women in the world.

McCaw looked at Alice saying, "I don't kid around with murder. Who's the lady in question?"

"Alice Roosevelt Longworth, daughter of President Theodore Roosevelt."

McCaw calmly wrote in his notebook. "Is that why so many bodyguards are hanging around and blocking up the aisles?"

"One of the reasons. My lawyer insists on the Pinkertons for my protection as well."

"Well, they're a nuisance, Miss Moon."

"Yes, they are, but unfortunately, needed."

"I see." Turning, he muttered under his breath, "Great. A bunch of swells." He waved to another officer to take Robert's statement.

Mona gave a faint smile. Detective McCaw retained a certain disrespect when it came to the rich. She knew how he felt.

"Are you the lead detective in this case?"

"I am, ma'am."

"It's miss. Remember, I am engaged to Robert Farley."

"Sorry, Miss Moon. I've been up for over twenty-four hours now. The Kentucky Derby brings a lot of riffraff to Louisville."

Mona bit her tongue as she felt McCaw's statement was a dig at her.

"I'm sure it does, Detective. How may I help?"

"Tell me what happened."

"Right after the race, we heard a woman scream and deduced it came from the box next to us."

"How could you single out this scream from the cries of the spectators?"

"A woman's scream that is fearful is a very distinctive cry."

McCaw nodded. "Who was screaming?"

"Mrs. Thompson."

"Where was she?"

"Standing next to her husband on his left, leaning over him."

"Then what did you see?"

"Mrs. Duff started screaming as well and calling for a doctor."

"Where was she?"

"Standing with her husband near Mr. Thompson."

"Did you see Mr. Thompson?"

"No, everyone was standing in a circle around him. It wasn't until we went over to help that we saw what the matter was."

"Who are *we*?"

"Dexter Deatherage went over first. Robert and I followed."

"How? Did you go around to their box?"

"No, we climbed over the railing."

McCaw shot a look at Mona's black and white dress with her white Derby hat and its black trim while making a notation. He also glanced at her black and white shoes. "Then what happened?"

"We pushed through the circle and saw Mr. Thompson hunched over in his seat. I attempted to check his pulse, but Mr. Deatherage stopped me. It was then that I saw the hat pin sticking out of his eye." Mona shuttered. "It was awful."

"Miss Moon, can you account for all your hat pins?"

"I can."

"May I see them?"

Mona bowed her head as McCaw counted them.

"How many hat pins had you started out with today?"

"Two."

"Describe them."

"Fourteen carat gold with a drop pearl top."

"Okay. Take a seat."

"When will we be able to leave?"

"When I'm finished with ya."

Another plainclothes detective came over and whispered something into McCaw's ear. "You're in luck. You can leave, Miss Moon, but I'll have to ask you not to leave town."

"You mean Louisville?"

"Yeah."

"I'm sorry, Detective, but I'm giving a party for Mrs. Longworth tomorrow. The governor is coming. I have to go back to Lexington. My guests had nothing to do with this."

"Oh, yeah?" McCaw thumbed over his shoulder.

Mona saw a policeman lead a stunned Willie Deatherage away in handcuffs with Dexter following close behind.

"What is going on? Why is Mrs. Deatherage in handcuffs?" Mona noticed Robert, Melanie, and Alice standing in a little knot watching Willie being led away.

Mona said dryly, "I guess I'll be staying after all, Detective."

3

Mona added, "You'll find me at the Seelbach Hotel."

Detective McCaw grunted, turned his back to Mona, gathering up his men.

Robert looked angry while Alice and Melanie seemed amused. Mona went up to them. "Ladies, I'll have my men take you back to Lexington, but I think Robert and I should stay."

"What about the party tomorrow?" Melanie asked.

Mona said, "We'll be back in time for the party. By then we should have this mess sorted out."

"Well, I'm staying," Alice said. "I'll come back with you tomorrow."

"If Miss Alice is staying, then I'm staying," Melanie announced. "I assume the hotel bill is covered by Moon Enterprises."

Mona closed her eyes for a moment, trying to keep from snapping at Melanie. "Very well, my men will escort you to the Seelbach. Robert and I are going to the police station." She motioned for her men to escort the women to the hotel.

"It's an outrage," Robert huffed, leading Mona to their car.

Mona gave her driver, Jamison, instructions to take them to the police station. A car filled with Pinkerton agents followed behind.

Mona said, "It was grandstanding for sure. McCaw can't seriously think Willie had anything to do with Thompson's murder."

"I'll make some calls and get this shut down."

Mona clasped Robert's hand as the car sped down the road. "We better wait, darling. Anything we do can have serious repercussions."

"What do you mean?"

"It might be chance, but we must consider this could have something to do with us."

"We've never met those people. How could it possibly involve us?"

"Surely, you've come across Thompson since you are in the racing business?"

"I know him to say hello and that's all."

"I remember the Duffs are invited to Alice's party tomorrow, so there is a connection."

"The racing business is a tight knit business, so I may have invited many guests that I don't know very well who are involved in the horse world."

Mona said, "That's what I mean."

"I don't see how this has anything to do with us."

"I'm not saying it does, but I am the head of a huge corporation. You are ninth in line to the throne of Great Britain. Alice Roosevelt, one of the country's most polarizing women, is staying in your home. She, alone, has a list of enemies a foot long. Maybe this was done to draw us in somehow."

Robert sighed. "You are right. I should have seen it myself."

The car skidded to a stop in front of the police headquarters. Mona and Robert hopped out and ran up the marble steps. A sergeant met them at the front door and escorted them down a dingy corridor to an office where Detective McCaw waited for them. He was smoking a

Romeo y Julieta cigar with his feet propped up on the desk and his hat tilted back on his forehead.

"Been waiting for you folks," he said.

"Detective, you are acting like every cliché I have ever read in a Dashiell Hammett novel," Mona said.

"Miss Moon, I'll take that as a compliment. I like his work," McCaw replied.

"Why did you think we would come? Your sergeant was waiting for us."

"Take a seat—both of you—please," McCaw said, adding the *please* as an afterthought.

Mona and Robert reluctantly sat down in two battered wooden chairs placed before McCaw's desk.

McCaw pushed a hat pin across the desk toward them.

Mona opened her purse and retrieved a handkerchief. "May I?"

"Be my guest. It's already been dusted for prints."

Mona gingerly inspected the hat pin which still had blood on it. She swirled it around by the tip.

"Do you recognize it, Miss Moon?"

"It looks like the hat pin that was sticking

from the eye of the unfortunate Mr. Thompson."

"Ever seen it before?"

Mona hesitated.

McCaw sat up in his seat. "Come on, Miss Moon. Just between friends here."

"Quit badgering Miss Moon. We came to see about Wilhelmina Deatherage."

"Lord Farley, do you recognize this hat pin?"

"No, I don't. I don't pay attention to feminine whatnots."

"But you do, don't you, Miss Moon?"

Mona bowed her head.

McCaw kept pressing. "Have you seen this hat pin before?"

"I've seen similar hat pins."

"Where?"

"I can't remember."

"Ah, Miss Moon, I'm disappointed in you. You've told your first lie."

Robert became agitated. "Look, what do you want from us? If Miss Moon says she can't place the hat pin, then she can't place it."

"I'm afraid she can."

Mona held up her hand. "He's right, Robert."

Robert's brow knitted together. "You can't

think we are responsible for that man's death."
He plucked a hat pin from Mona's hat and held it
up. "See, Miss Moon's pin doesn't look anything
like that pin."

"I took note of everyone's pin this evening at
the Derby. We recorded fifty hat pins from
women sitting around Mr. Thompson. As for you
two, I wanted to see if either of you would throw
your friend, Wilhelmina, under the bus, to save
yourselves. I already knew this was the hat pin
Mrs. Deatherage was wearing today."

"Lots of women have that type of hat pin,"
Mona said.

"No, they don't, Miss Moon. This blue and
green enamel hat pin was designed by Charles
Horner, a famous English jewelry designer, and is
rare. Mrs. Deatherage already told me that it was
her mother's. She was wearing two hat pins today
and has only one in her possession now."

Mona said, "If you search Churchill Downs
you will find many hat pins on the premises.
Women lose pins all the time. They simply
become loose and fall from the hats. That's why
we usually wear more than one hat pin, especially
on windy days. My goodness, there were over

sixty thousand people at Churchill Downs today."

"We have searched the grounds and have found thirty-four hat pins, twenty-five cuff links, none of them matching, two wallets, none with money, various tortoise shell combs and lipstick tubes, seventy-two dollars in change, two pocket watches, four wrist watches, and several pairs of women's panties. I don't even want to think about how or why the ladies' panties were discarded."

Mona leaned forward. "See. Willie's hat pin could have fallen from her hat and someone picked it up."

"That's our theory until we find something else."

"You will let Willie go?"

"She has been released and is on her way home with her husband." McCaw felt his chin. "He socked me, you know. Got a nice right hook for a lawyer."

"Did you have to humiliate Mrs. Deatherage by putting her in handcuffs in front of everyone?" Robert asked, angrily. "Did you think that itty-bitty woman would overpower your gorillas escorting her from Churchill Downs?"

"I'm saying that the eldest son will inherit the bulk of Robert's fortune and the title. The British operate under the primogeniture system of male inheritance. Men get it all."

"If the death taxes don't force me to sell the estate after Father dies," Robert added.

"We'll get into your father's financial status in another conversation, Robert. It does need to be addressed, but what I'm trying to say to Mona is that other children may inherit a portion set down by the parents, but not anything having to do with the house, land, or title."

"What if we just have girls?" Mona asked.

"Then everything will go to the eldest daughter except the title, if a male relative does not contest the will, but Robert's line will die out then. Of course, there are incidents of a daughter inheriting the estate and a male relative receives the title if he signs away his monetary rights."

"I'm stunned. I don't know what to say," Mona said, looking perplexed.

"You said there were more issues," Robert said, his brows knitted together.

"Unfortunately. This is what really upset your father, Robert. It's the Moon name."

Mona looked wide-eyed at Robert. "Oh, gosh, I forgot about that."

"What are you talking about?" Robert asked.

"Let me help with this, Mona." Dexter turned to Robert. "In order to accept the Moon fortune, Mona had to agree to certain stipulations. Unusual requests."

Robert asked, "What kind of stipulations?"

"Nothing illegal or immoral I can assure you. Like the British, Manfred Moon was trying to keep the Moon fortune and name intact for future generations."

Robert sat at the edge of his chair. "Get on with it, man."

"Mona had to agree she would live at Moon Manor and run Moon Enterprises. Unless she did so, she would lose the inheritance. This is the kicker that your father is having a hissy over, and I don't blame him."

"For God sakes, man. Out with it." Robert looked concerned.

"Mona has to keep Moon as her last name, regardless of marriage, and her husband also has to legally change his last name to Moon and go by that name publicly. If Mona reneges on this, then the fortune and control of Moon Enterprises will go to Melanie."

Stunned, Robert said, "I don't know what to say. This is a legal mishmash for both Mona and myself."

Mona looked downcast. "My head says one thing and my heart another. One thing is for sure, Robert cannot be disinherited. We must call off the wedding, at least until we find a legal solution to this issue."

Dexter nodded. "I don't see a way around this. One of you has to relinquish your position."

"Well, it's not going to be Robert." Mona pulled off her engagement ring and handed it to Robert. "I will not be the cause of your disinheritance."

Robert pushed her hand away. "Don't be daft, you silly cow."

"I insist, Robert."

"Be quiet, Mona. No one is doing anything until we've examined this further. You go on and plan the wedding. Dexter and I will try to find a way out of this conundrum."

"But what about your father?"

"I'll handle him."

"Have you two set a date?" Dexter asked.

"Late fall," Mona said. "I wanted to meet with Robert's father first. We had planned to go to England in July."

Dexter said, "I would let that visit go for now. If Robert's father sees intent to marry, he might go ahead and disinherit in a fit of pique."

Mona shot a look at an agitated Robert. "Yes, I see that."

"And Robert," Dexter said.

"Yes?"

"Keep your temper intact. No rushing off belligerent telegrams. No hateful letters. Let your father cool down. Go about your business. I'll handle this."

"Make sure you do, Dexter," Robert said.

"That's why I get paid the big bucks."

Mona put her hand on Robert's arm. "I have faith in Dexter. If anyone can see a way out of this mess, it will be Dexter."

Robert grabbed his hat and helped Mona to her feet. "You'll be in touch, Dexter?"

"Sooner than you think. Willie and I are having dinner with you two tonight."

"Great. Just great," Robert said sarcastically,

before escorting Mona out of the office.

Mona felt a chill walking out of the Moon building. What if she lost the man she loved? Would she be willing to give up the Moon fortune to marry Robert? Would she?

11

"I don't see what the problem is, Mona," Willie said as they were taking a turn about the garden. "You love Robert, so marry him."

"This is more than about me. I employ hundreds of men and women who support thousands more. I can't just drop everything because I want to marry Robert. If I leave, Melanie will run Moon Enterprises into the ground. That woman has no business sense. For once, my employees are making good money. Productivity has gone up. No strikes. People making good money spend money. It helps local economies. If Melanie gets in control, the first thing she'll do is cut wages, and then she'll slash the budget for new equipment and repairs. Safety will become an issue, and people will get hurt. She'll downgrade the employees' benefits and programs I've established. She'll undo everything I have done. I just can't walk away. There's a lot at stake besides my own personal happiness."

"People say that you are a socialist or worse—a communist."

Mona laughed. "I believe people should pull themselves up by their bootstraps, but sometimes a person needs a helping hand. I don't mind giving that helping hand as long as they land on their feet. After that, they are on their own. I would refer to myself as a benevolent capitalist. Come on, Willie. You can't deny that the system is rigged against certain groups, especially women. No matter how brilliant or accomplished we are, women always get the crap end of the financial stick."

"Wait until Robert's father dies, then marry."

"I'm not going to ask Robert to change his last name. He would become a laughing stock in his own country. I won't do that to the man I love."

"There's got to be a way out of this to satisfy everyone."

"I keep hoping and praying."

Willie said, "There's Dexter and Robert now. Oh, dear. Robert looks like he has swallowed a sour pickle."

Robert came over and kissed Mona on the lips and then greeted Willie. "Dexter and I had a serious conversation about this matter."

"Any solution?" Mona asked.

"Every idea we came up with causes one of us to lose our inheritance, but we'll keep trying." Robert looked down at his casual clothes. "Sorry, but I didn't dress for a formal dinner. Not in the mood."

"The kitchen is grilling vegetables and chicken. Strawberry shortcake for dessert. Fast and simple. We are going to eat in the garden."

Robert replied, "That's fine, but I warn you that I'm in a foul mood. Not fit company for ladies such as yourselves."

"We'll bear up somehow," Mona said. "Come on. Samuel has set lemonade and snacks at a table until dinner is ready."

"I can smell dinner now," Dexter said. "Making my mouth water."

"Good. Monsieur Bisaillon is letting Obadiah and Jedediah prepare dinner. He thinks I don't know the lads are putting their own twist on the grilling, and Monsieur is hoping they will fail."

Willie said, "That's not very nice."

"Monsieur Bisaillon is not a nice man, but a great chef. He's always worried about his job, which makes him difficult for the rest of the staff," Mona confided.

They sat down at a metal table with a clear pitcher of lemonade filled with ice and ginger cookies. Mona poured everyone a glass. "Salute."

The four friends clicked their glasses together.

Mona took a long sip as she was thirsty when Willie twitched. "What is it?"

"You'll think I'm silly."

"No, I saw you realize something and then shrug it away."

"It seems like the solution to your problem is so simple, but if it was, Dexter would have thought of it."

Dexter said, "What is it, dear?"

Willie looked attentively at them. "Don't laugh."

"We won't," Robert assured, good-naturedly.

"Why can't Mona be a Lucy Stoner and Robert hyphen his name?"

Mona drew back. "Lucy Stone!"

"Who the bloody hell is Lucy Stone, and what has she to do with us?" Robert asked.

Undaunted, Willie continued. "It seems to me that Manfred Moon was and Robert's father is trying to protect property for future heirs. It really has nothing to do with Mona or Robert. It has to do with their children."

"Go on, darling," Dexter encouraged.

Willie gulped. "Mona keeps her maiden name after marriage and gives up the title of 'duchess.'"

Mona turned to Robert. "That's a Lucy Stoner."

"And Robert hyphenates his name to Farley-Moon or Moon-Farley. All of Mona's children have rights to Mooncrest Enterprises since it is a family firm, and Robert's title and property go to his eldest son who relinquishes any claim to the Moon money. Manfred decreed that Mona's children had to have the last name of Moon, and Mona's husband was required to legally change his last name to Moon. He never said anything against a hyphened name did he, Dexter?"

"Let me think on this, Willie. You are throwing something new at me," Dexter said.

"I don't think it will work, Willie," Robert added.

"Why not? The British royal family did it."

"How do you mean, Willie?" Mona asked.

"Come on now. Don't have such short memories. Before 1917, the British royal family was named Saxe-Coburg and Gotha. You can't tell me that's a real last name. It sounds like noble houses joining together for a single dynasty."

Mona looked to Robert. "It's true. The House of Windsor is a made-up name."

Robert sat back in his chair and thought for a moment. "What do Melanie's children go by?"

Dexter answered, "They have the same issue, but Melanie never had a title to deal with. All Manfred was trying to do was keep the Moon family name alive after his death. There were no males to carry on the family line, so Manfred was determined the family name would pass through the females."

"But what did Melanie do?"

"She had her two children's last names legally changed to Moon, and she kept her maiden name after her divorce," Dexter said.

"I don't think my father will go for it," Robert

said. "And I want Mona to have the title of duchess."

"I don't care about a title," Mona said.

Robert said, "You don't understand, Mona. The title has much to do with protocol—where you stand before the king, where you are seated at a banquet, or how you are presented at court. We would not be equals."

Mona grew irritated. "How many times in the last ten years have you visited King George at Buckingham Palace or even talked with anyone from the royal family? David will have to marry when he inherits the throne, and Bertie already has two daughters, Elizabeth and Margaret, who will one day grow up and have children of their own. There will be no shortage of heirs to take over the British throne. I don't think our children will ever be in danger of being king or queen."

"Things will be different when I am duke. I will have responsibilities. I just can't abandon my life in England. I have people relying on me."

Irritated at Robert's stubbornness, Mona sniped, "You've done a good job of avoiding that for three years since you've been living here."

"Cheap shot, Mona."

"The world is changing, Robert. Customs and traditions are breaking down. You being a duke will not be what it was before the Great War."

"My estate is still the largest employer around for twenty miles. I can't just do as I please during a depression because I want to get married—and to an American at that."

"Let's not forget that it's been American money from American heiresses who have saved the British aristocracy for the past fifty years."

"Golly gumdrops, Mona. Are you implying that I am marrying you for your money? You must be daft."

"Mona. Robert. Both of you calm down," Willie admonished, looking anxiously at the two of them.

"You don't think I am going to pack up and move to England, leaving everything behind here, do you?" Mona asked. "To tell you the truth, I think this whole notion of estates and titles is rubbish. That way of life is dying. And what's my being an American got to do with anything? If you think I'm going to bow and scrape before your snobbish friends, think again. We Americans fought a war to be free of English tyranny."

"This English way of doing things has served my country well for over a thousand years, and you are living in the exact same system, my dear. You Americans copied from us."

"I work for a living. I don't make my income by collecting rents from hard-working farmers tilling my land while sitting on my "aristocratic" bum."

"It seems to me that you own—how many thousands of acres in the Bluegrass alone? Sounds like the pot calling the kettle black."

"My employees make above the average pay grade and have benefits. Can the men and women who slave on your father's estate say the same thing?"

"The English are a great people. After all, the sun never sets on the British Empire."

"Really? Do you think the native people in India and Rhodesia are thrilled with British rule?"

"Steady on, you two," Dexter advised.

"Oh, this is impossible," Robert said, rising from the table.

Mona snapped, "Where are you going, Lord Bob?"

"Away from you." Robert marched over to

his house through the pastures.

"You rascal!" Mona shouted. "Come back and fight." Furious that Robert walked away from her, Mona stormed into Moon Manor slamming the back entrance door.

"Did I cause this ruckus?" Willie asked, perplexed.

Dexter shook his head. "It's two high-spirited Thoroughbreds who needed to release some tension. We've seen them go at each other before. Mona and Robert are both scared to death that they are going to lose each other because of silly technicalities. The argument was a bad case of nerves. Mona and Robert are both sensible people. They'll work this out."

Willie looked up. "Ah, look, Samuel is bringing out dinner. What shall we do?"

"I intend on eating it. As far as I'm concerned, their leaving means more food for us."

"I'll talk to Mona before we leave."

"You'll do no such thing, darling. Leave her be. You and I are going to enjoy this wonderful meal and then go home. And for what it's worth, your ideas to solve this are stupendous. Very creative."

"You really think so?"

"I do, and as soon as I get you home, I'll show you how well I think of your ideas," Dexter said, winking.

"Then let's have Samuel put the food in a doggie bag and skedaddle."

"Another splendid idea from the creative mind of Wilhelmina Deatherage."

Willie blushed and kissed her husband. She was so lucky to have him.

Mona watched from her bedroom window as Willie and Dexter left while she mulled over Willie's advice. She thought it had possibilities if refined. She had to make Robert see that being a duchess meant nothing to her, and the whims of two old men should not come between them.

But when going to bed, Mona fell asleep thinking about what Natasha Merriwether had to do with Cody and Helen Duff, finally dreaming of Rusty Thompson with a hat pin sticking out of his eye trying to say something to her.

As hard as she tried, Mona couldn't make out what Rusty was saying.

It bothered her.

12

A rustling on the balcony woke Mona up, and she turned on her nightstand light.

"Turn that bloody thing off," Robert said, coming through the balcony double doors.

"I wish you'd come through the front door like a normal person rather than like a cat burglar. You have a key to the house."

"This is more romantic, don't you think? A sort of Romeo and Juliet rendezvous."

"Yeah, and look what happened to them."

Robert picked up Chloe, who was snuggled next to Mona and moved the dog to her little bed on the floor. Chloe yawned and gave a little yelp of protest.

"Did I wake you?" Robert asked.

"Yes, but I knew it was you. Otherwise, Chloe

would have been barking her head off, and the Doberman watchdogs would have seen to you."

"I met those dogs on the way here. New, aren't they? They cornered me until your man came and gave the command to release me."

Mona chuckled. "Our midnight assignation has been outed. My reputation will never recover."

Robert pulled back the covers. "Move over, Mona. I'm simply knackered."

Mona turned over and faced Robert, leaning on her elbow. "Where did you go, Robert?"

"I went to my club and had a chin wag with the lads." Robert turned to face Mona. "I had a club soda. I didn't drink if that's what you're thinking."

"It's been a stressful day."

"And I made an ass out of myself blowing up like that. I'm afraid, darling, that is my nature. I have a filthy temper. One of my many faults that you're just going to have to get used to."

"I think we were both stinkers. I'll apologize if you apologize."

Robert held out his pinky finger. "Forgive and forgiven."

Mona crooked her pinky finger with Robert's. "Forgive and forgiven."

"Good, now I need sleep." Robert fell back on the pillow and pretended to snore.

"Robert, what did you and the guys talk about?"

"It was mostly tittle-tattle, but I did hear gossip about Rusty Thompson."

Mona shook Robert's shoulder. "Don't hold out on me. Give."

Robert laughed. "I knew that would pique your interest. You do love your puzzles, don't you?"

Mona sat up in bed and tickled Robert.

"Oh, stop, Mona. I hate being tickled," Robert said, laughing.

"Shush, Violet will hear you. Even she would wake to your snorting."

"Then stop, you wicked woman. I'll tell you."

"I'm waiting." Mona threatened to tickle Robert again.

Robert sat up. "There are no legal charges against Rusty Thompson for horse tampering, and they are probably not coming. The racing commission was investigating until rumors of threats against some members on the board squashed the investigation."

"Do you think those rumors are real?"

Robert shrugged.

"What did Rusty do?"

"Usually when owners or trainers go rogue, they dope their own horses if they are the favorite and then bet against them, but Rusty was caught doping a horse that he had no association with. The owner caught Rusty with a syringe in his horse's stall at Latonia."

"Who was this owner?"

"Rumor has it, and I emphasize the word *rumor*—Ed Bradley."

"Ed Bradley! What was Thompson thinking?" Mona mulled this information over.

"What are you thinking?"

"You never mind."

"No, really."

"I was thinking that Violet may be right, and we have James Cagney to thank for it."

"James Cagney? What does a movie star have to do with this?"

"According to Violet, everything. Now go to sleep," Mona said, winding up her alarm clock.

"I'm setting it for five."

"Five?"

"You know the rules. You sneak in after ten—you have to be gone before sunrise."

"The servants all know I visit you at night."

"Yes, but if they don't see you, they don't have to deal with it. They can put their hand on the Bible and swear they saw nothing."

"Hypocrite."

"I can't do anything that would hurt Moon Enterprises, so I must be chaste in the public's eye."

"Fraud."

"Yep.

"Come here, Fraud."

Smiling, Mona turned out the light.

13

Taking a break from work, Mona and Dotty went to the Phoenix Hotel for tea. Dotty wanted a cold drink and tiny cakes while Mona wanted to snoop. She was hoping they would run into the Duffs or the Merriweathers, but they bumped into Alice Roosevelt in the lobby instead.

"What are you two doing here?" Alice asked, looking surprised.

"We needed a reprieve from business correspondence and decided upon tea," Mona replied.

Alice smiled. It wasn't a real smile, more like a smirk that said, "I know you're lying, but I'll go along."

"So, here we are," Dotty said, brightly.

"I came down for tea myself. Please be my guests," Alice said. "I hate to have tea alone."

Mona said, "That would be lovely. Thank you."

Dotty said, "Yes, thank you, but I think you shall never be alone, Mrs. Longworth."

"You'd be surprised, my dear."

As Mona and Dotty followed Alice into the dining room, loud laughter sounded as the doorman threw open the doors for two incoming guests. Mona swirled around to catch Cody Duff and Natasha Merriweather dash inside from the rain, giggling and arm-in-arm.

Alice leaned over to Mona. "Mrs. Merriweather should be more discreet. A woman can have an affair as long as there are no overt signs. Rumors are one thing. Sticking one's extramarital affairs in everyone's face is another." Alice looked around. "Here's a good table. Right by the window. Now we can watch people come and go."

"They can't be having an affair," Dotty said, sitting down and putting her things in the spare chair. "Mrs. Merriweather is old enough to be that boy's mother."

Alice motioned to a waiter. "That *boy* is breaking his wife's heart by associating with Mrs.

Merriweather in such a public way."

"Tell me more," Mona encouraged.

"Cody's room and mine are on the same floor. Only two nights ago, I heard a terrific row in the hallway. It was Helen and Cody Duff."

Dotty's eyes widened. "Do tell."

"They were coming back from dinner, and the argument must have started in the elevator where it spilled out into the hallway. Helen accused Cody of improprieties and said she wanted them both to go back to Texas where it was clean."

"Improprieties and not adultery?" Mona quizzed.

Alice said, "That was the exact word she used. Why? What's the difference?"

"Most women would use the word cheating or adultery when accusing their husbands of being unfaithful. She could have meant something else."

Alice waved her hand in dismissal at Mona. "If I know women, and I do, the woman meant adultery."

"I'm getting close to Mrs. Merriweather's age," Dotty said. "I would love it if a young man in his twenties paid attention to me."

Alice looked Dotty over. "My dear, you have more of a chance of getting killed by an ax murderer than having some young buck sniffing around."

Mona bit her lip to keep from laughing at Alice's audaciousness, but did manage to say, "Does that include you, Alice?"

"Of course, it does. I'm talking more about myself really." She looked at Dotty tearing up. "Oh, my dear, pay no attention to me at all. I'm just an overbearing old biddy. I'm spoiled rotten and have no discernible talent other than being famous, but you are of use to the world. I'm a throw-away. You don't know how lucky you are to be needed."

Stunned by Alice's self revelation, Mona felt kinder to her. "Yes, Dotty is a mainstay for me. She is of great help."

Insulted by Alice's view of her, but somewhat soothed at Mona's praise, Dotty asked, "What else was said?"

"Just Cody replying that Helen didn't know what she was talking about, and he and Natasha were just friends."

"Don't they always say that?" Dotty said, unfolding her napkin.

"Is that all you heard?" Mona asked.

"The slamming of their door. Oh, wait a moment. Helen said that Cody's mother was going to cut off their allowance if Cody didn't straighten up. Then Cody yelled back, 'I knew you didn't marry me for my manners and good looks.'"

"He's not that all-in-all. I've seen better," Dotty said.

"I think he might have been sarcastic, Dotty," Mona said, softly.

"Yes, I see that," Dotty replied sheepishly, watching a waiter pour hot tea into everyone's cups. "Might I have a ginger ale, please? Bring me a separate glass of ice with the ginger ale. I'll do my own pouring."

The waiter nodded and departed.

"Anything else you might have noticed?" Mona asked, innocently, raising her cup to her lips.

"You are a cheeky devil, Miss Mona. I knew you didn't come to the Phoenix to have tea. You are on a scouting mission."

"Are we, Mona?" Dotty asked, looking around. "How divine."

"We did need a break, but if I should discover

something to help my friend, Mrs. Deatherage, then so much the better."

Alice picked up her teacup. "It must be nice to have a friend like you, Mona."

"Don't you have a pal?" Mona asked, laughing, but when she saw that Alice didn't answer, Mona felt sorry for her. She realized the pranks, the parties, the affairs were a mindless diversion for an intelligent woman who hadn't the courage nor the discipline to forge an introspective life. Alice didn't want to be alone with her thoughts. She liked the chaos—the controversy. It kept her from thinking.

Dotty leaned over the table. "Don't look up, but Mr. and Mrs. Duff walked in."

"They've spotted us," Alice said. "Now the fun begins." She waved to them.

"Good afternoon," Mr. Duff said, guiding his wife to the table.

Alice nodded and replied, "Good afternoon to you both. Just come in out of the rain?"

"We were looking at property. Lexington is such a pretty town, we thought we might give it a go," Mrs. Duff said.

Mona thought that was strange as Mrs. Duff

seemed so supportive of Helen, who wanted to go back to Texas. Maybe they weren't so close after all.

Alice asked, "We just started tea. Would you like to join us?"

Mr. and Mrs. Duff looked at each other.

"Yes, we'd like that," Mr. Duff said, getting a nod from his wife. "Perhaps something stronger as well?"

"Pull up a chair," Dotty said, removing her things from the spare one. "Mrs. Duff, sit here."

"We don't want to intrude," Mrs. Duff said.

"You're not," Mona reassured.

Alice motioned to the waiter to bring more teacups.

As the waiter brought more cups and lovely plates of bite sized cakes and sandwiches, Mr. Duff ordered a scotch and water.

There was a moment of awkward silence until Mona asked, "What property were you interested in?"

Mrs. Duff said, "We've been looking at the north side of town since we'll probably be getting an apartment in Cincinnati as well."

"You'll love the Cincinnati Art Museum. My

husband's family donated the land for it, you know," Alice said before biting into a cucumber sandwich.

"Oh, I wasn't aware," Mrs. Duff said, her hand fluttering to her throat.

"And the Taft Museum used to be the Longworth's family home. You must visit there as well," Alice continued, trying to look innocent.

Mr. Duff, angry at Alice's lording her aristocratic connections over them, remarked, "Isn't it funny the Longworth family home is now the Taft Museum? Most people think it was the home of President Taft."

"It belonged to Taft's sister-in-law who married his half-brother," Alice replied, stiffening.

"I guess the Longworth and Taft families must have been very close. It would explain why your husband supported William Howard Taft running as president instead of your father. Must have caused some very interesting conversations between you and your husband at the dinner table."

Alice bristled and her eyes took on a dark countenance.

Before Alice could erupt, Mona said, "We saw

Cody and Mrs. Merriweather come in together."

Mrs. Duff looked uncomfortable. "They must have been at Pennygate. They are co-owners of a horse and go out every morning to watch its training."

"Oh, I didn't realize," Mona said. "I wish them the best of luck. I no longer race my horses, but I let others board their mares and foals with me."

"Why is that, Miss Moon?" Mr. Duff asked.

"I love the business of horse racing, but I don't know enough about it yet to get in the game. Besides, there are aspects of the sport I don't like."

"Such as?" Mrs. Duff asked.

"The corruption for one thing," Mona replied.

"Yes, I know what you mean," Mrs. Duff said. "We were petrified when learning about Rusty Thompson's charges. I wish we had told the Thompsons that they were uninvited for the Derby."

"But Mr. Thompson was never charged with anything," Dotty said.

"He was being investigated by the racing commission," Mr. Duff said. "He was caught red-handed with a syringe in a stall with a horse that he had no connection with. It was only a matter of time before the man was thrown out of the business."

"Mr. Thompson still managed to garner enough support to have the investigation halted," Mona said. "Many thought he had been set up."

Mrs. Duff said, "We are like you, Mona. We want to play the game, but don't know enough to know whom to trust. I'm afraid we made a misstep with Rusty Thompson."

"I hear gangsters are involved somehow," Dotty said.

"From where?" Mona asked.

"The beauty parlor," Dotty said.

"Oh," Mona said, dismissingly. "It seems the Merriweathers are throwing themselves headlong into the fray."

"Mrs. Merriweather is an heiress—old money." Mr. Duff turned to Alice. "I'm surprised you don't know her, Mrs. Longworth."

"I never said I didn't know Natasha."

All eyes swung to Alice.

"It seemed you two didn't know each other when I introduced them to you at the party," Mona said.

"You didn't. You were talking to the Deather-ages," Alice said. "The Merriweathers never came through the receiving line."

"We did," Mrs. Duff said.

"Yes, but not the Merriweathers," Alice said.

"That's right. How odd," Mrs. Duff said. "I never noticed."

"That's correct." Dismayed, Mona rubbed her forehead. "I must have a false memory of introducing the Merriweathers. So you do know Natasha from before?"

"Long story," Alice sniffed.

"How did you meet the Merriweathers?" Dotty asked of the Duffs.

Mr. Duff said, "We were introduced to them at a charity ball in Houston. I already knew her father since we had business dealings together. We discovered that we both had an interest in Thoroughbred racing and the Bluegrass. This seems to be a town where one's past or lack of lineage doesn't matter as long as one has money. I hate to put it bluntly like that, but there it is."

"I know what you mean," Mona said. "You would think that, but it's tough to break in with the aristocratic set here."

"What do you mean by *aristocratic set?*" Mrs. Duff asked.

"The original pioneer families who are hanging on to their land—and I mean barely," Dotty said. "They run the social aspects of the city, although they lost political control decades ago, but the names of Clay, McDowell, Breckinridge, Warfield, Todd, or Morgan still have cachet in this town."

"I know Mary Breckinridge quite well," Mona said.

"What's she like?" Mrs. Duff asked.

"She's a fabulous woman," Mona replied.

"She's the daughter of a traitor," Mr. Duff said.

Mrs. Duff looked nervously around the table. "You must excuse my husband. His family is originally from southern Illinois bordering Kentucky. Some lost Confederate soldiers stumbled onto his family farm killing his grandfather and seriously injuring his father."

"They weren't lost. They were deserters," Mr. Duff snapped angrily, his face taking on a thunderous look. "They murdered my grandfather in cold blood over a mule, abused my grandmother, and caused grievous harm to my father. He finally succumbed to his injuries caused by those ruffians, leaving behind a young widow and me, barely nine. My grandmother only spoke of the incident once, but she knew their names and their hometowns. Apparently, those men stayed for days terrorizing my family, if you can call them men—more like animals. I've been looking for them ever since. They may still be alive."

Mrs. Duff said, "You should see my husband's collection. He has files upon files and every imaginable artifact he can find from the war."

Mona thought it doubtful that the deserters could still be alive after all these years, but she thought Duff's anger, though justified, ventured on obsession. It amazed her the war still affected so many people to this day. She remained silent, reflecting on the enormity of the Civil War, and all the lives destroyed by its aftermath.

Holding up her teacup, Alice said, "We can agree that Breckinridge was a traitor, especially since he served as Vice President for the U.S. right before the Civil War, Mr. Duff. He might have been president if Stephen Douglas and John Bell hadn't split the Southern vote in 1860. It's what caused Lincoln to win."

Mr. Duff nodded to Alice.

"And yet you've come to live in a Southern town, Mr. Duff," Mona remarked.

"Most people here are transplants like yourself, Miss Moon. I don't intend to associate with the Confederate rabble," Mr. Duff said.

Alice laughed, "You are a kindred spirit. Sir, I drink to your health. Never was a more stupid war fought."

Dotty said, "Lexington was split on the Civil War. Kentucky was a slave-owning state, but never declared its allegiance to the Confederacy. It stayed with the Union."

Nibbling on an egg salad sandwich, Mrs. Duff said, between bites, "It's hard to fathom that our grandparents and parents lived in an era where it was thought to be morally right to own human beings as property."

"I have many employees at Mooncrest Farm who are descendants of slaves. They tell me stories handed down through oral tradition. My butler, Mr. Thomas, has a slave ancestor who was first brought here in 1799. I think their stories would make an insightful book," Mona said.

Mrs. Duff asked, "You have a Northern accent, Miss Moon. How did you come to Kentucky?"

"My family is from Kentucky, but I grew up in New York City. After my uncle died, I came back to live in the ancestral home, which is Moon Manor."

"How do you find it?" Mr. Duff asked.

Mona laughed, "You're putting me on the spot, Mr. Duff, but I'll answer. I find the Bluegrass area to be one of the more beautiful spots I've visited, and I have traveled the world. The pace is slower, which I like. I love Appalachian quilting, crafts, and folk art which I now collect. Very ingenious people in the mountains. I agree the people can be standoffish, but once they get to know you, they are warm and willing to give you a hand when you need it. I didn't think I was going to like this region when I came and wasn't sure I could make a go of it, but I have grown to love the area. I think Lexington is going to grow into a cosmopolitan city, and I want to grow with it."

"Did you have any ancestor who fought in the Civil War, Miss Moon?" Mr. Duff asked.

"I had family who fought on both sides, Mr. Duff."

"How did you get to Texas, Mr. Duff?" Dotty interrupted, wanting to divert the conversation away from Mona and the Civil War. The war was still too raw and fresh a memory for people as almost everyone had an older relative who had been maimed or killed in the war. It was not a subject for polite conversation because arguments always ensued.

Mona gave Dotty a slight nod of thanks.

"Needed a job, so went wildcattin'," Mr. Duff answered. "Just some dumb luck when I hit a vein of black gold."

"Luck for us," Mrs. Duff joined in. She reached over and held Mr. Duff's hand.

"I wonder how Mrs. Thompson is doing?" Dotty asked.

"I hear she is back at her home in Lexington. She's keeping a low profile. Are you going to press charges, Mona?" Mrs. Duff asked.

"I don't want to harass a grieving woman, but I think Mrs. Thompson needs to be evaluated by a psychiatrist. She might still be dangerous."

Both Mr. and Mrs. Duff raised their eyebrows.

Alice stood. "This has been grand, but I am retiring for a nap."

Mona folded her napkin. "Yes, it's been lovely, but Dotty and I still have a few hours of work before dinner yet. So nice to see you both again, Mr. and Mrs. Duff. Alice, thank you for the tea, but we must be off."

Dotty gathered their things and followed Mona into the lobby. They stood for a moment putting on their wraps, watching Alice take the stairs while the Duffs waited for the elevator.

Mona was ready to leave when she spied someone she knew emptying ashtrays.

"Go on and wait for me in the car, Dotty. I shan't be too long."

"Okey dokey," Dotty replied, glancing about the lobby. What or who took Mona's interest at the last moment? That's what she wanted to know.

14

"Hello, Jellybean," Mona said to the small man dressed in a housekeeping uniform.

"Get away. You're blowing my cover," Jellybean hissed.

"What are you doing?"

"Hit the road!"

"Tell me what you're up to and I'll go away."

"I'll meet you in the mezzanine in a few minutes. Now beat it, kid."

Mona went outside to her waiting car and told Jamison to take Dotty back to Mooncrest Farm. "Don't worry about me. I'll catch a ride with the boys," she said, referring to the Pinkertons in the car behind hers. She waved goodbye and went back inside the Phoenix Hotel and up to the mezzanine.

Sitting in a comfy chair, she picked up a copy of the morning newspaper and read it as were several other men who were in town for business. After several minutes, Jellybean came up to notify one of the men he had a phone call and that he could take it in the lobby. The other gentleman, seeing the only other person on the mezzanine was a woman, wondered if Mona was a lady of ill repute and decided to read the paper in his room where he would be safe from Jezebels.

Once the men left, Jellybean approached Mona. "May I get you anything, Miss?"

"How about a Tom Collins and some information?"

Jellybean glanced about. "Never, never blow my cover like that again."

"I'm so sorry. I thought you had gotten a second job to make ends meet. It was stupid of me, of course."

Jellybean appeared placated. "What do ya want?"

"Why are you working in housekeeping?"

"The hotel management hired me to catch a thief. Someone's pinching towels from the maids' carts, ashtrays from the lobby, personal effects from several of the rooms."

"Everyone takes the towels and ashtrays. They consider them souvenirs."

"Not this amount. The Phoenix had to double their orders on towels, matchbooks, and ashtrays. The management thinks it's someone staying for an extended period of time."

"As exciting as chasing down a thief of matchbooks sounds, it doesn't have anything to do with me, so I'll be going."

"Beneath ya, huh? Look over the railing at two gentlemen reading the paper. One is wearing white spats. Go on. Look."

Mona drifted over to the railing and casually looked down at the two men Jellybean described. She sat back down in her seat.

"Did you see them?"

"I did. One of them is seriously trying to look like George Raft ten years ago."

"Know who they are?"

"You're dying to tell me."

"They are from the Chicago Outfit, Capone's gang."

"Thus the gangster look. Isn't Capone in prison for tax evasion?"

"Yep."

"When did they check in?"

"Right before the Derby."

"And they still haven't left?" Mona pondered for a moment. "You heard about Rusty Thompson's murder at the Derby?"

"Yep."

"You think these guys had something to do with it?"

"Possibly, but they are more likely to shove a blade between the ribs. There are rumors Thompson was mixed up with Capone's boys."

"Why do you think they are here, Jellybean?"

"Besides stealing ashtrays and towels which they are sending back to their relatives for a gag? I think they are here to announce to the horse community that they are moving in and taking a piece of the pie. They are sure making a big splash about town."

"I guess since Prohibition has been relaxed, the gangs need to find other sources of income."

"And expanding gambling is on the table."

"Who are they?"

"Hoppy Giunto and Antonio Lolordo."

"Does management know who they are?"

"The gentlemen registered under their given names."

"Is the management going to do anything about them?"

"Not unless they want the hotel to mysteriously burn down."

"And what is your job exactly?"

"To get proof they are stealing from the hotel and keep an eye on them."

"I don't envy your job. Sounds like it might be dangerous."

"Nobody pays any attention to a little black man puttering about unless they want something. To white folks, I'm invisible."

"I heard Rusty was being investigated for tampering with a horse. You know which horse and the owner? No one in my circle is saying."

"That's because it was kept hush hush before the Derby. Might have thrown the race." Jellybean began dusting the end tables.

The silence grew as he ignored her.

Mona grew impatient, knowing that Jellybean liked to toy with her. She pulled a fiver from her purse and put in on the coffee table. "Tell me or I'm going to complain about the service in this hotel, naming you."

Jellybean grinned, knowing Mona was blowing smoke. He loved jousting with her, as Mona was one of the few white people who was always square with him. "It was Ed Bradley's horse, and it was Ed Bradley who caught Thompson."

Mona pretended she didn't already know this information. "Bazaar? Bazaar as in the Kentucky Derby contender for this year?"

"Ed Bradley won the Derby in 32 and 33. He had a good chance of winning this year. No one in the history of horse racing has had a run like Ed Bradley. I think Thompson was there to kill Bazaar. Put that in your pipe and smoke it."

"Thanks, Jellybean. Catch up with you later." Mona hurried out of the hotel and jumped into the car waiting for her. All she muttered to the driver was, "Idle Hour Farm."

15

Mona was shown into the conservatory where Edward Bradley was tending to his beloved orchids.

"Mona. What an unexpected pleasure. Are you here for a chat about the charity event?"

"I'll come right to the point, Ed. Did you catch Rusty Thompson trying to dope Bazaar?"

Rattled at Mona's bluntness, Bradley blinked heavily before recovering his composure. "Sit down, please. May I offer you a lemonade or perhaps something stronger?"

"Quit stalling. I want an answer."

"Young people today. So impatient," Bradley muttered to himself. "If you won't sit, I will. This will take some time to explain." He sat down in a wicker chair.

Mona pulled one up close to him. "I don't mean to come across as interfering with your private affairs, but is the rumor true?"

"It is," Bradley said, reluctantly. "I wanted to keep it quiet before the Derby, which is why I didn't press charges. I didn't want it to get into the newspaper. You must understand news of this nature could have thrown the race off."

"I understand, but you did report it to the racing commission."

"Not formally. Just bent a few ears of men who owed me favors. I wanted Rusty Thompson thrown out of the business. People of his ilk give racing a bad name."

"I think the racing commission was finished with its investigation. Robert heard through the grapevine that some members of the racing board had been threatened and dropped the inquiry."

Bradley's brows knitted together and his left hand trembled a bit. "I hadn't heard that, but it doesn't surprise me."

"This is why I stopped my horses from racing. I hate the corruption in the sport."

"Not everyone is crooked, Mona. Take it from me. If you run an honest operation, there is nothing like seeing your horse fly across the finish line. It's one of the biggest thrills you can get—taking a small foal and turning it into a champion." Bradley leaned back in his wicker chair and seemed lost in his memories for a moment.

Mona tapped on the arm of Bradley's chair. "What was in the syringe?"

"A concoction of cocaine. It was at Latonia Race Track. I went to check on Bazaar before bedtime when I discovered his guard was missing. That's when I discovered Thompson. I hit him with my cane and held him off until grooms and trainers from other outfits came running."

"Other people saw this?"

"Yes."

"Why haven't they spoken up?"

"I paid them not to. Again, I didn't want to throw off the Derby. If news got out it would have had a tremendous negative effect. Throw doubts upon all the horses racing."

"Why did Thompson do it?"

"He told me that he was approached by gangsters out of Chicago. They wanted Bazaar out of the running for the Derby."

"Why didn't he say no?"

"You know why. He didn't want his legs broken or his wife beat up or worse. Ever since parimutuel betting is on the table, horses are being doped up like never before, and there is pressure on horse owners from the mob. They see parimutuel betting as a way to make up for the profits lost from bootlegging."

"How are they sure this type of betting is going to pass the legislature?"

"It will. Don't you doubt it."

Mona thought for a moment. "The plan was to dope Bazaar and then have him taken out of the race the next day after he was tested for drugs. When he showed positive for drugs, you would be disgraced and Bazaar would be disqualified from running in the Derby."

Bradley didn't respond.

"Did you always check on Bazaar before the day of a big race?"

Bradley nodded.

"My question is why didn't he leave when he saw you? He could have just pushed you down and run. You said you hit him with your cane and held him off until the others came running.

Again, why didn't he run? Why were you two fighting?" A chill came over Mona. "Tell me, Ed, was the syringe for Bazaar or for you?"

Bradley didn't answer.

Mona thought back to her party. "I always assumed Mrs. Thompson was pointing the gun at Willie Deatherage, but was she?" Mona stood up and played as though she was pointing a gun at Bradley. "But if I remember correctly, you were sitting at a table that was in her line of fire. She said, 'You killed my husband,' but to whom was she speaking?"

"I remember the incident very clearly."

Mona dropped her arm. "Was she speaking to you, Ed? Were you the one she was really pointing a gun at? I know about your past. You weren't exactly a boy scout."

"I knew the moment I met you, Mona Moon, that you had a first-rate mind. I'm sorry that I'm so old or I'd give Robert a run for his money. He's not good enough for you."

"Enough of your blarney. Stick to the story."

"You're very close to the truth. Capone's boys came to visit me. Said they wanted me to throw the Derby race. Hold Bazaar back. I told them they could go to the Devil. That's when they decided to play rough."

"Your death was to be a warning to other horse owners either to play ball or strike out."

"Precisely."

"You've got guts, Ed. No one can doubt that about you." Mona looked at Bradley with new affection. Even at his advanced age, the man was still playing life by his own rules. "Who do you think killed Thompson?"

"The mob, no doubt. He failed in killing me, so he had to pay the ultimate price for failure—his life. What better signal to send everyone in the horse business than to murder one of their own at the Kentucky Derby."

"Ed, I gotta ask."

"Stop right there, missy. I know what you're going to say next. Rest easy. Bazaar ran a clean race as did the other horses. Cavalcade had a great day. Let's not take that away from him or Isabel Dodge. The better horse won."

Noticing that Bradley looked tired, Mona said, "Thanks, Ed. I best leave you to your orchids."

"You still in for my charity event?"

"Wild horses couldn't keep me away."

Bradley sighed. "Yeah, funny."

Mona sniffed. "I thought it was amusing."

"Mona."

"Yes?"

"One more thing. If Thompson's murder goes south for those boys, they'll be looking to rid themselves of any potential witnesses. Watch your back."

"I always do, Ed. I always do."

16

Mona was resting in her bedroom before dressing for dinner.

Monsieur Bisaillon had thrown a little temper tantrum about the lack of decorum at Moon Manor and insisted that he be allowed to serve more ceremonial dinners as all great houses did. The possibility that Mona might become a duchess with her engagement to Robert Farley had thrown her staff into a tizzy. Windows were washed, floors buffed, silver polished, rugs aired, hedges trimmed, fences painted, and Mona was expected to do her part.

It was true that Mona had been dressing less and less formally for dinner as she was hoping that she could ease out of that tradition. Sometimes she felt like rummaging the refrigerator with Violet and eating in the kitchen. She found the European tradition of formal dinners every night to be a huge time suck. She had better things to do with her evenings, but Mr. Thomas gently explained that the servants felt standards were slipping. In other words, the help was embarrassed by Mona.

To keep peace in the house, Mona agreed to five nights of formal dining and two nights of eating in regular day clothes. It was a compromise everyone could live with, but Mona felt Bisaillon was a tyrant. Although it did open her eyes that her employees, especially those who worked at Moon Manor, expected Mona to act as a grand lady.

In keeping with tradition, Samuel rang the gong every night at seven giving Mona an hour to dress, and the servants time to eat their dinner before serving hers.

The house telephone rang. Mona picked it up. "Yes? I see. Tell him I'll be down in a moment and have him wait in the front drawing room. Do we have any sandwiches left over from afternoon tea? Bring him a tray of some of those, a piece of coconut cake, and lots of hot coffee. I imagine this is not a social visit. Thank you, Mr. Thomas."

Mona hurriedly dressed in a long-sleeved, high-necked, blue velvet dress. The bodice sparkled with diamond-shaped glass beads, reflecting the light. In addition, Violet had laid out a diamond brooch and bracelet.

After slashing on lipstick, Mona checked herself in a full-length mirror. "Goodness! I look like a Christmas tree." Resigned that Violet thought she needed to step up her game like the rest of the house staff, Mona unlocked her bedroom door and went downstairs with Chloe at her side.

"Good evening, Detective McCaw."

Popping an egg salad sandwich into his mouth, McCaw stood while simultaneously chewing and wiping his mouth with a napkin. "Excuse me, Miss Moon, but I haven't eaten anything since lunch. This tray was very good of you."

"Think nothing of it. I don't like to see food go to waste. My chef always makes more than enough."

"So it would seem."

Chloe whimpered and wagged her tail at the Detective.

"Please don't give Chloe any food. I'm trying to teach her not to beg and, as you can see, she needs to lose a pound or two."

Detective McCaw reached down and petted her. "I'm partial to hunting dogs."

Seeing that she was not going to receive a treat, Chloe went in search of one in the kitchen where Thomas or Samuel might take pity upon her.

"Why are you here, Detective?"

"I am going back to Louisville tonight, and I wanted to tell you Wilhelmina Deatherage is no longer a person of interest. We do think Mrs. Deatherage innocently lost her hat pin and someone picked it up."

"Mr. Thompson's death is considered a murder of opportunity then and not first degree?"

Detective McCaw didn't respond.

Mona regarded McCaw's silence. "Detective, you didn't come here to tell me that."

"It was to warn you, Miss Moon."

"Warn me, Detective?"

"My men saw you watching two men at the Phoenix Hotel, who we consider armed and dangerous."

"You think gangsters from Chicago had something to do with Rusty Thompson's death?"

Ignoring Mona's question, McCaw said, "After you left the Phoenix Hotel, you drove straight to Idle Hour Farm to see Ed Bradley."

"Are you having me followed?"

"We were following the two thugs who followed you to Bradley's house. I must say, Miss Moon, your bodyguards are incompetent. They should have spotted those goons trailing you."

"I should have spotted them myself, Detective." Mona went over to the bar. "Would you like a drink? I'm going to pour myself a bourbon."

"No, ma'am."

Mona sat opposite McCaw with her drink. "Please continue eating."

Detective McCaw sat back down and picked up another sandwich. "What did you and Ed Bradley talk about?"

"I'm sorry, but you need to talk to Ed about this. I don't like to betray a confidence."

"Did he tell you that he was attacked by Rusty Thompson with a syringe full of a cocaine solution after he told the Chicago boys "no"

148

about throwing the Derby race?"

It was Mona's turn not to reply.

"Miss Moon, I don't think Rusty Thompson's death will be the last if we don't lock up who's responsible. I've already interviewed Mr. Bradley, and that's the story he told us. I just need you to confirm that he told you the same. That's all."

"He did."

"Now that you've been made, be careful, Miss Moon. These men are ruthless. My guess is they spotted you surveilling them at the hotel."

"Obviously, I need to brush up on my sleuthing skills."

McCaw picked up some sandwiches and put them in his pocket. "For my men in the car. You don't mind, do you?"

"You will find that your men have received a picnic basket full of food and hot coffee for the ride back to Louisville. My butler, Mr. Thomas, overlooks nothing. Have a pleasant journey home, Detective."

McCaw was halfway across the room when he turned and said, "I usually don't make comments like this, but you are the spitting image of Jean Harlow."

"You like Jean Harlow?"

"I saw her at your garden party. It's like you two could be identical twins."

"I'm taller."

McCaw shook his head. "It's the damndest thing. You sure you two aren't related?"

"Positive."

"Hmm. I see." McCaw doffed his hat. "Goodbye, Miss Moon. Thanks for the sandwiches."

"Goodbye, Detective. Safe passage home." Mona walked Detective McCaw to the front door and watched him leave. Turning to Samuel, she said, "Have Obadiah come to me. I'll be in the library."

A moment later Obadiah stood before Mona.

"Do you know Jellybean Martin?"

"I know him when I see him."

"I want you to get a message to him tonight. Tell him that Chicago is on to him. He'll know what it means. Take Jedediah with you and don't stop until you find him. Here's ten dollars in one-dollar bills for tip money."

"You mean bribe money, Miss?"

Mona grinned. "If Jellybean is not working at the Phoenix tonight, start with the doorman at the hotel. Doormen know everything."

"What about dinner?"

"Samuel will pinch hit for you both tonight. Now skedaddle."

"Yes'am." Obadiah's face lit up at the possibility of adventure. He couldn't wait to tell his brother. They were going to have a night out on the town.

Mona went into the formal drawing room where Robert was waiting in white tie, shirt, and vest. He pulled at his starched collar. "I thought I was done with this nonsense when I left England. Couldn't I just wear a suit?"

"The servants are making a stink. They want us to project a certain aura of respectability."

"They are worried about their reputation in comparison to my father's staff. They are making a fuss about nothing. My father's servants are more snobbish than my father and rude to anyone lower in rank, including myself. Your employees are polite, efficient, and clean. We can barely get our cook to wash her hands before preparing a meal. As far as I'm concerned, your house staff is superior in every way."

"There's nothing wrong with employees wanting to show off a little. The least we can do is to acquiesce. Let's not let them down."

Mona took Robert's arm as they moved to the dining room where Mr. Thomas had laid out Moon Manor's best china and gleaming silver with a massive yellow and white floral arrangement in the middle of the table. She hid her dismay at the formality of the place settings as she knew the table had taken much work and time. "Putting on the Ritz" was a much bigger deal than she had thought. Mona smiled and said to Mr. Thomas and Samuel, "Everything looks lovely. Thank you for such a beautiful table."

"Since Obadiah and Jedediah have been sent out on an errand, I will be helping serve the meal, and Dora is helping Monseiur Bisaillon in the kitchen."

Mona could hear the rebuke in Mr. Thomas' voice, but decided to ignore it. "Very good." She let Samuel pull out her chair and settled in for the two hour long meal. Looking down the table at a miserable Robert sitting at the other end, she mouthed, "Let the games begin." Then she rang a sterling bell that was crafted into the form of the Roman goddess of agriculture, Ceres.

Dinner had commenced.

17

"I'm sorry I'm late," Mona said breathlessly, entering Dexter's office.

"We haven't been waiting long," Dexter said, pointing to a chair sitting opposite Mrs. Thompson and her lawyer.

Mona nodded at them while taking off her white cotton gloves with pearl buttons around the wrist. "I've come as requested."

Mrs. Thompson's lawyer cleared his throat. "We appreciate that you have agreed to meet with us."

"You're here to ask me to drop the charges against Mrs. Thompson."

"Yes, but Mrs. Thompson wants to tell her story of what happened that day. Once you've heard it, I think you will see Mrs. Thompson is more victim than aggressor."

"I'm open to anything clearing this up, but I cannot have your client pointing loaded pistols at myself or my friends. I'm sure you understand."

Mrs. Thompson said, "Miss Moon, if you agree to drop the charges, I will go to my sister's in Maryland. There's nothing for me here anymore."

"When will you go?"

"I can leave as soon as this matter is put behind me, otherwise, I'm trapped here."

"How do I have your assurances that you will leave, Mrs. Thompson?"

Dexter said, "Mrs. Thompson will sign an affidavit confirming her intent to relocate plus sign a confession of firing a gun at your party, with details as to how and why."

Mona leaned back in her chair. "I see." She turned to Mrs. Thompson. "I have some questions."

Mrs. Thompson nodded. "Go ahead and ask."

"Was there an insurance policy on Mr. Thompson?"

"Yes, but I haven't applied for it. The insurance company won't give me the money until

Rusty's murderer is caught. They consider me a suspect."

"How much is the policy?"

"Three thousand."

"Who is the beneficiary?"

"I am, of course."

Mona didn't reply that Mrs. Thompson might get another shock regarding her husband's life insurance. "When you came to my house, who was the object of your anger?"

"To tell you the truth, Miss Moon, I don't remember much of that day. I remember being worked up. I was very upset and traumatized by my husband's death."

"You had no intended target?"

"I don't remember who I was going to shoot, and that's the God's truth. I'll swear to it on the Bible."

"What's the last thing you do remember clearly about that day?"

"Natasha Merriweather had come to the house to check on me."

"Natasha was at your house?"

"Yes."

"Tell me about her visit," Mona said.

"I was surprised to see her. After all, she was going to your party, and after the Derby mess, I'd thought she never wanted any further contact with me."

"Was she dressed for the party?"

"Yes."

"What time was this?"

"About two, I guess."

"What did you talk about?"

"She said she was horrified about Rusty's murder, and I should call on her for anything that I needed."

"Did she talk about Willie Deatherage?"

"She badmouthed her quite a bit."

Dexter stiffened.

"Does Natasha think Willie killed your husband?"

"She said so," Mrs. Thompson replied.

"Do you?"

Mrs. Thompson shook her head. "Not really. At first, I thought so after the police confirmed the murder weapon was her hat pin, but I don't see how she could have. I was sitting right next to Rusty. I would have seen her. And what would be the motive? We are not acquainted with the

Deatherages. Never have been." She opened her purse and pulled out a handkerchief.

"Were you standing and watching the race?"

"Everyone was."

"Including your husband?"

"I assume so. He would have to stand to see the race."

"But you don't specifically remember?"

Mrs. Thompson shook her head.

"Any suspicious characters in the aisle?"

"No one stood out, but the aisles were crowded with people."

"Mrs. Thompson, are you aware that your husband was being investigated by the racing commission?"

Mrs. Thompson bowed her head and whispered, "Yes."

"Your husband attacked Ed Bradley with a syringe filled with a cocaine solution."

"But the matter was dropped," Mrs. Thompson's lawyer added.

Dexter asked, "Why was that?"

"We don't know," the lawyer replied.

Mona asked, "Did your husband tell you of the attack?"

"No, and I don't want to know what happened either."

Dexter took notes on a legal pad. "How did you find out?"

"Some men came to the house, and I heard them talking to Rusty."

"What men?" Mona asked.

"They were from the racing commission, telling Rusty that he was in serious trouble. Ed Bradley had launched an informal inquiry."

Mona thought back to the Derby. "It wasn't in the papers, so how did you and Willie have an inkling of this, Dexter? You mentioned something at the Derby about Rusty," Mona said.

"You can't keep something like attacking Ed Bradley or Bazaar quiet. I'm sure one of the men, who witnessed the attack, said something and the rumor got started around town. I heard it from my barber."

"Ed told me that he paid everyone to keep quiet," Mona said to Dexter.

Dexter shrugged. "People talk, Mona. What can I say?"

"Why would your husband do such a thing?" Mona asked.

"I don't know. Things became muddied after Natasha hired Rusty. He wasn't himself. He was agitated and worried."

Mona remembered Natasha had said she was thinking of hiring Rusty Thompson and had not hired him officially. "About what?"

"I don't know." Mrs. Thompson looked frantically about the room. "I swear I don't."

Mona continued. "Your husband was known for cutting corners."

"So does everyone in this business. Rusty never did anything the other trainers don't do," Mrs. Thompson replied, defensively.

"I doubt they attack one of the leading horsemen in the country, Mrs. Thompson."

"I don't know what came over Rusty. He was never a violent man, and he loved horses. This attack was not in his nature. He never gave me a reason why. 'The less I knew, the better,' he said." Mrs. Thompson wiped the tears from her eyes.

"Mrs. Thompson, would you like a glass of water?" Mona asked, pitying the woman.

"I need for this to be concluded one way or another. My future preys heavily on my mind."

"If you would bear with me, I have a few more questions," Mona said.

"Please go ahead," Mrs. Thompson said, wearily.

"Let's go back to Natasha Merriweather's visit. Can you go step by step? You heard the doorbell and opened the door."

"As I said before, I was surprised to see Natasha. I let her in. She said she was checking on me before going to your party for Alice Roosevelt. I replied it was very kind of her."

"Did you know Natasha well?"

Mrs. Thompson's eyes widened. "No, that's what was so puzzling. I knew her to speak with her, but that's all. She had hired Rusty to purchase horses for her."

"When was this?"

"Four months ago, I think."

"And the attack on Ed Bradley was two months ago."

"Just about."

"Then what happened?"

"She saw I was having a cup of coffee and asked if she could have a short one. I went into the kitchen and poured her one, asking if she took cream or sugar. She replied that she took it black. I went back into the living room and gave it to her. That's when my memory gets fuzzy."

"Could you see Natasha from the kitchen when you went for the coffee?"

"No."

"So, you couldn't see her?"

"Well, the coffee pot was on the stove. I had to turn my back to pour it."

"I suppose your cup was in the living room still?"

"Yes, I left it on the magazine stand. It's one of those little tables that swivel and can store papers and magazines."

"I have one of those in my library." Mona paused for a moment. "Is that all you remember?"

Mrs. Thompson rubbed her forehead. "Everything gets blurry after that. I remember Natasha stayed for a bit, but I don't remember her leaving, and I don't remember how I got to your party, Miss Moon. You've got to believe me."

"Your car was parked off the road beyond Lord Farley's farm."

"I DON'T REMEMBER!"

"Whose gun was it?"

"It was Rusty's. He purchased it about four months ago. Said it was for protection."

"Where is the gun now?"

"The police confiscated it."

Mrs. Thompson's lawyer intervened. "My client is tired and needs rest. She has answered your questions truthfully."

"I see." Mona cast a glance at Dexter.

He nodded.

"I will drop the charges, Mrs. Thompson, if you sign and abide by the agreement Mr. Deatherage has drawn up. I have no wish to have you prosecuted. In fact, I'm terribly sorry that you have had to go through this ordeal. I want you to understand that I have an obligation to keep everyone around me safe, including myself."

"I understand, Miss Moon. I had no idea of what I was doing. I'm so ashamed."

"I am satisfied that you acted under duress." Mona stood and shook Mrs. Thompson's hand. "I wish you well, Mrs. Thompson. I leave you with Mr. Deatherage. He will handle things from here on out. Good luck to you."

"Thank you, Miss Moon." Mrs. Thompson

looked relieved and her lawyer smiled at her.

Mona gathered her purse and gloves, leaving Mrs. Thompson alone with the two lawyers. She was off to find the Duffs.

18

She found the couple in the bar of the Phoenix Hotel, having a glass of wine. "May I join you?" Mona asked. Startled, the Duffs looked up as they were caught unawares, but quickly recovered.

"Miss Moon, what a pleasant surprise," Mr. Duff said, jumping up to offer Mona a chair.

"Thank you," Mona said to Mr. Duff, who scooted her chair in. "I just finished at my lawyer's office and thought I'd catch a cool drink before heading home. I was hoping I would run into someone I knew."

"Lucky for us," Mrs. Duff said. "May I order you something?"

"Iced tea would be refreshing, with lemon on the side, please."

As Mr. Duff went to the bar, Mrs. Duff said,

"I hope your visit with your lawyer was for a happy purpose. I keep waiting to see your engagement to Lord Farley announced in the papers any day now, but nothing as of yet."

"We are going to make it official after I meet his father."

"Oh, you've never met him?"

"No, I haven't had the pleasure, but I want to get his blessing before we officially announce."

"He doesn't approve?"

"He doesn't approve or disapprove. He's never met me." Mona gave Mrs. Duff a gracious smile. "The British have their own way of doing things."

"I see. I must say Lord Farley is a handsome devil and so charming. He could charm the feathers off a bird."

"Thank you. I find him rather charming myself."

"Who's charming?" Mr. Duff asked, returning from the bar.

"We were discussing Lord Farley."

"Oh, yes, congratulations on your betrothal."

Mona said, "Thank you. We're happy."

"When's the wedding?"

"I was just telling your wife that I plan to meet Lord Farley's father, and we'll set a date after that."

"Gotta get the old man's approval, eh?" Mr. Duff said, beckoning to the waiter to place the iced tea in front of Mona.

Mona laughed, "I guess you could say that."

Mr. Duff held up his wine glass. "Here's to a happy marriage and a long and contented life. I hope you'll be as happy as Mrs. Duff and I. Won the prize when I married her."

Mrs. Duff beamed at her husband's praise.

"I'll drink to that, Mr. Duff. Cheers," Mona said, clinking their wine glasses. She took a sip of her iced tea before asking, "Have you found any property that you like?"

Mrs. Duff said, "We've seen everything available on the north side of town and beyond, but nothing that we cotton to. I'm thinking we should go back to Texas and try again next spring."

"Do you agree, Mr. Duff?"

"I'm thinking we should push ahead, but my wife gets what she wants. If she says we're to go back to Texas, that's what we'll do."

"You have a very agreeable husband, Mrs. Duff. Not all women are so fortunate. If you return to Texas, will Cody and Helen be going with you?"

"I know Helen will. Her family lives in Houston."

"Not Cody?"

His florid face turning redder, Mr. Duff answered bluntly, "He has purchased an interest in Pennygate Farm, so he'll probably stay to keep an eye on his investment."

Embarrassed, Mrs. Duff looked down at her lap.

It was obvious they thought their son was having an affair with Natasha Merriweather, but what could they do but ride it out and pretend it wasn't happening. "I have a question to ask both of you."

"Go ahead," Mr. Duff said.

"At the garden party, you mentioned that you knew about Rusty's indiscretions. How did you know? It wasn't common knowledge as it hadn't been reported in the papers."

"Let me think," Mrs. Duff mused. "I believe it was Natasha who warned us."

"Yes, that's right. She said he was caught doping a horse, and he was going to be thrown out of the horse business."

"Were you going to hire Thompson?"

"Yes. In fact, it was Natasha who first suggested him, but came back a month later and told us not to do so. We had gone to several Thoroughbred auctions with him and were ready to sign a contract," Mr. Duff said.

"Who invited him to the Derby?"

The couple inquisitively looked at each other as they tried to remember.

Mrs. Duff said, "It had to be the Merriweathers as we didn't. In fact, we were quite surprised when we saw them in our box after what Natasha had told us."

"Oh, you came separately to the Derby?"

"We came to Louisville the night before. The Merriweathers came directly from Lexington with the Thompsons and arrived before us. I should have asked Mr. Duff to order the Thompsons out of our box, but I didn't want to cause a scene. I was very confused that the Merriweathers brought them after warning us not to associate with Rusty. I wish now I had. Our good name is forever associated with Mr. Thompson's death.

We'll never live it down."

"Did you come to my party separately as well?"

"Why yes. We met up in your driveway. Is there something wrong? All these questions," Mr. Duff said.

Mona smiled reassuringly and glanced at her watch. "Oh, my goodness. Look at the time. I must be going. It was great to run into the both of you again. Well, too-da-loo."

Mona hurried out of the hotel and motioned for Jamison to pull the car up.

"Where to, Miss Mona?" Jamison asked.

"Home. Dotty is waiting for me. I have a pile of correspondence to go through."

"Yes'am."

Mona settled in the back seat, piecing together who said and did what. At the moment, all roads were pointing at Natasha Merriwether, but she was nowhere near Rusty Thompson when he died. Mona was positive.

But then again, Mona had been watching the race.

Had Natasha moved closer to Rusty Thompson?

That was the million dollar question.

19

Mona was holding hot dogs over a fire Robert had made in his backyard as he came out with a tray.

"Did you bring the mustard?" Mona asked. "I like mustard and onions on my hot dog."

Robert held up the mustard, relish, and a bowl of chopped onions. "I didn't forget, Babycakes." He laid the tray on a side table near Mona. "Dogs done yet?"

"I think so." Mona swung the stick toward Robert to pluck them off and place in buns.

He put the required condiments on them before sitting on the ground next to Mona.

"Here ya go."

Mona took a bite. "Hmm, that's good." While chewing, she lay her head on Robert's shoulder.

"Darling, you're making it hard for me to eat."
Mona sat up. "So sorry."

Robert scooted closer and put his left arm around Mona. "That's better. I'm holding my dog and my tootsie wootsie at the same time. What could be better?" He took a large bite covered in mustard, relish, and onions. "Oh, golly, that's good. A needed break from all those heavy French sauces and syrupy compotes Bisaillon has been throwing at us."

"It's good to get away from all that formality." Mona snuggled closer to Robert.

"This is so nice. Just the two of us—not having to watch what we say in front of the servants."

"How was your day?"

"Good, I think. I met with Mrs. Thompson."

"Are you going to prosecute?"

"I think not. I felt sorry for her, Robert. This whole ordeal must be so traumatic."

"You said you think not. What's going to be the deciding factor?"

"As soon as we confirm that she has signed my attorney's agreement and gone to her sister's in Maryland, then Dexter will call the DA and inform him I'm not interested in pursuing this."

"It's for the best, I think."

"I do, too. Besides, she claims she doesn't remember coming to Moon Manor."

"Do you believe her?"

"Oddly, I do."

"Why?" Robert asked, sliding another hot dog on a stick to be roasted in the fire.

"You may think this strange, but I think she was poisoned."

"Poisoned as in "to die?"

Mona roasted another one as well. "No, I think she was given something to make her act out."

"Explain."

"Every lead about Rusty Thompson's murder lands at the foot of Natasha Merriweather. She visited Mrs. Thompson right before our party for Alice."

"So?"

"Natasha was coming directly here after her visit, but asked for coffee as Mrs. Thompson was already having a cup. My guess is that when Mrs. Thompson went to fetch another cup, Natasha put something in her coffee to make her irrational."

"What else?"

"It was Natasha who had some kind of working arrangement with Rusty Thompson—not the Duffs. She recommended him to the Duffs and then acted as though she had fired him because of the Bradley incident, but how did she know about it? Ed said he paid everyone to keep it quiet, yet she referred to the incident at the party. How would she know unless Rusty told her? I think Natasha is mixed up in all of this, and she put something in Mrs. Thompson's coffee."

"Pretty flimsy."

"Here's another thing. This is something men don't think about, but women do. It is forty-five minutes on a good day from Mrs. Thompson's house to Moon Manor, and yet, Natasha asked for coffee."

"I don't follow."

"There is no restroom available from Mrs. Thompson's house to Moon Manor. Unless she had an iron kidney, a woman wouldn't have asked for coffee. It's a diuretic. She'd ask for water."

"You're reaching."

"Let's take Violet for instance. If she drinks coffee, she's looking for a bathroom within fifteen minutes, and she's a young woman. Natasha is middle-aged."

"That's Violet."

"I'm telling you most women don't drink coffee if they are not going to be near a powder room."

Robert threw up his hands, "Okay. Okay. I'm a believer. Just don't go around and announce your theory in public. You have no proof."

"You don't think I'm as stupid as that?"

"Sorry. I'm just on edge with this murder, and now my father acting like an ass. I feel like our lives are on standstill because of the wishes of two old goats—my father and your dead uncle. I'm very frustrated."

"Not making any headway, huh?"

Robert gave Mona a squeeze. "My father's lawyers are being impossible, but don't worry about it. I'll take care of it."

"Can we throw some money at this?"

"I won't deny the estate is in trouble. It's not due to mismanagement, but American farmers are more efficient, and they have taken British farmers to task with wheat and corn prices. Once, those markets were dominated by the British, but you colonists have beaten us with lower prices. We can't compete."

"Like I said, can't we throw some money at this? Doesn't your father expect a dowry anyway?"

"I don't want your money, Mona. It will make me look like a fortune hunter. I have my own money inherited from my mother, but it's not enough to get the estate out of the red. We need new equipment, irrigation, and seed for the pastures. Oh, did I tell you my father said the manor needed a new roof? The list goes on and on."

"How about a loan of a hundred thousand dollars to be paid back within thirty years with zero percent interest?"

"That's a ridiculous loan. Even on those terms, I'm not sure the estate could pay it. Once my father passes to the Great Beyond, I will have to pay death taxes. I'll be in arrears for years. Ah, it's a bloody mess, Mona. I'm not bringing anything to this marriage, but debt and my filthy temper. You better shuck me."

"Not on your life. You made a promise to marry me, and I'm making you stick to it. Besides, we are both hot-tempered. We'll have to work around our natures."

"Forgive and forget?"

"Forgive and forget." Mona held out her pinky finger which Robert clasped with his and shook hardily.

"Let's talk about something else. Discussing my father's estate depresses me."

"I think we should look upon these problems as adventures—our brains and hard work against insurmountable odds. Remember Mooncrest Farm was operating at a loss when I took over, and I turned that around. We'll turn your estate to the black as well."

"That's because people were fleecing the Mooncrest coffers. I don't think that's a problem for me."

"How do you know? Are you sure the cook isn't 'cooking' the books, and then reselling food on the side and putting the money in her pocket?"

"I love it that you are trying to help, but let's get my father to agree to our marriage first, and then I'll turn you loose on restoring my ancestral farm." Robert moved his finger across his heart. "I swear."

Mona crooked her finger and replicated the same move over her heart. "Agreed."

They snuggled together watching the moon rise over the treetops while discussing their future, but every so often, Mona would glance over her shoulder.

She just couldn't shake the feeling that something wicked was coming her way.

20

Mona was coming out of the Mooncrest Building in downtown Lexington when she bumped into Natasha Merriweather.

"Hello, Mona," Natasha cooed.

"Hello," Mona said, somewhat cautiously, looking around for her bodyguards. They were smoking and reading the morning paper in their car. Only Jamison saw the encounter and pulled the car up, honking the horn.

Upon hearing the car horn, Natasha pouted at the disruption. "I'm so glad I've bumped into you. I have a proposal for you, but I see you're ready to leave."

"How may I help you?" Mona said, not wishing to be rude, but wary of Natasha.

Natasha put her arm around Mona. "Not in

public like this, dearie. Let's go to the ice cream parlor on the next street. I'm dying for a root beer float. We can cut through the alley. Tell your man to meet us there. The alley is too small for your car."

Mona mouthed to Jamison to meet her on the next street and gave him a secret signal that she might be in danger.

Jamison barely nodded and pulled out into the street.

Giving her attention solely to Natasha, Mona extracted her arm away from Natasha's clasp on her and put her hand in her coat pocket. "You wouldn't have been waiting for me, were you, Natasha?"

"I've been caught. I did see you go into the Mooncrest Building. I hope you are not cross," Natasha said, hurrying up the alley. "Come on, Mona. You're lagging behind. Ice cream awaits us."

Mona stopped and acted as though she was checking her stocking seams. "Coming," she said, reaching inside her purse.

Natasha stepped away as two men moved out of a shadowy doorway.

Mona quickly pulled the gun from her purse, surprising the two men and Natasha.

When Natasha shifted, Mona turned the gun on her. "Don't even think about it." She wagged the gun and said, "Over there with your boys, Natasha."

"There's three of us, Mona. You can't hold us off."

"Maybe, but Jamison says otherwise."

Natasha and the two men swung around to see Jamison standing behind them with a double barrel shotgun. Seeing they were outgunned, the men dropped their weapons and held up their hands.

"Isn't this a pretty box of pickles," Mona said. "You two must be Hoppy Giunto and Antonio Lolordo."

One of the men grunted.

"I'll take that as a yes. Now, which one of you wants to tell me what was your intent? I don't think it was to beat me up. Too public a place as I can see we are starting to gather attention." She waved to several people who had stopped at the opening of the alley and were watching.

"Shall I call the police?" one man called out.

"Thank you, but no," Mona shouted back. "I've got this under control."

"What now?" Natasha asked, her face red as a beet.

"We are going to the ice cream shop—the four of us and talk this out over a banana split. You're buying, Natasha." Mona put her gun back in her purse and strode past Natasha and the two men. "Well, come on. No dilly dallying. You've been made."

The two men looked skeptically at each other, shrugged, picked up their guns, and followed Mona with Natasha trailing behind—not happy. Not happy at all.

21

Mona filled a spoon with whipped cream and sucked it dry. "Heaven." She looked around at the three sour people sitting with her. "Aren't you going to try your sundaes? No? Then I'll take a cherry. I love the cherries." Mona scooped a cherry from Natasha's chocolate sundae.

One of the men groused, "I'm glad the boys are not here to witness this humiliation."

"Don't men in Chicago eat ice cream, Mr. Giunto?"

Mr. Giunto flipped back his hat. "See. That's what we wanted to talk to you about."

"Just talk?" Mona asked.

"How come you know our names? And we hear you've been asking a lot of questions about Rusty Thompson. We don't like that."

"Did you two have anything to do with Rusty Thompson's death?"

Giunto said to his partner, "There she goes again. Poking her nose in our business."

"So you did kill him?"

Giunto threw his napkin down in disbelief. "Ain't you got some nerve, lady. We came down here to find out what happened. We thought you might know."

"You came all the way from Chicago to see what happened to a horse trainer? I suppose out of the goodness of your heart."

"Yeah, we did," Lolordo said, cricking his neck. "What makes you think we are from Chicago?"

"With that accent, you're certainly not from Boston or New York."

Lolordo said, "Wise guy, huh?"

"Are you saying that you weren't ordered to put a hit on Rusty Thompson?"

"You're asking dangerous questions, lady. But if we were, we certainly wouldn't use a women's hat pin in front of a horse track full of sixty thousand witnesses. You capiche?"

Giunto added, "We'd plug him with a .38."

"Shut up," Lolordo said. "You talk too much."

Giunto looked sheepishly around. "No one heard me."

"I heard you, you dumbbell."

"What did you want with me?" Mona asked.

Lolordo said, "We just wanted to ask a few questions. That's all."

"Really?"

"Maybe scare you a little bit. We don't like you pokin' around."

Mona glanced at the man's sundae. "You'd better start working on that. It's starting to melt."

Both men plowed into their sundaes. Giunto looked up. "Hey, this is good. Be better with a beer chaser."

Mona glanced at Natasha. "Don't you like your root beer float?"

"I'm not hungry."

Mona put down her spoon. "What's your connection with these two mugs?"

"I don't know what you mean. I've never seen these two men before in my life."

"Natasha, you are in this mess up to your neck. Connect the dots. Everywhere I turn, your name comes up."

"I had nothing to do with Rusty Thompson's murder."

"But these two are here at your behest."

Natasha shook her head. "No, they are not."

"Lower your voice, please and smile," Mona said. "We're suppose to be enjoying our ice cream."

Natasha nervously sipped a little of her float while Mona happily finished her sundae.

"This has been swell, but I think it's time you gentlemen packed up and head back to Chicago. My chauffeur has contacted my lawyer, and I'm sure a phone call has been made to the FBI." Mona glanced out the window. "I see my body-guards are stationed outside—finally."

Lolordo groused, "Lady, you need to get new bodyguards. They stink." He stood and motioned to Giunto.

"I'm not finished with my ice cream," Giunto complained.

"You are now. Come on."

Giunto doffed his hat. "Ladies, enjoy the rest of your afternoon."

Natasha shuddered as the men left the ice cream shop. "I'll be going, too."

Mona put her hand on Natasha's arm. "We are not finished."

"Yes, we are."

"You're going to answer some questions, or I'm going to tell Alice Roosevelt about your involvement in this. Alice doesn't seem to like you, and you both run in the same social circles. Now if Alice buried a voodoo doll of Nellie Taft in the White House lawn, what is she capable of doing to someone like you? I imagine she would make a few phone calls, and your reputation would be gone." Mona snapped her fingers. "Just like that."

"I'm not involved in any murder."

"What about the attack on Ed Bradley?"

"Again—I had nothing to do with it."

"The Duffs said that you told them about the charges against Rusty Thompson. Since it wasn't in the papers, how did you know he was being investigated?"

"I overheard some jockeys talking about it."

"You're lying, but let's proceed. How did you get mixed up with the mob?"

Natasha lowered her head. "I gamble. Got in over my head. They knew I was interested in

Thoroughbred racing and was coming to the Bluegrass to purchase property. To pay off my marker, I was told if I did certain things it would be paid off."

"What were you told to do?"

"I was told to hire Rusty Thompson."

"And?"

"And for me to milk him for information."

"What kind of information?"

"Anything. You know how people talk. They wanted to know if I heard of any stock tips, business moves, horse purchases—anything that might give them the edge to make money."

"If you were in debt to the mob, how could you pay for a horse farm?"

"My father owns it. He thought it would be a good investment. Listen, Mona. My parents are elderly. It would kill my father to know that I gamble. When he passes, I get his estate and can pay off anything I owe. I'm playing for time until that happens. I don't want my father to know about—" Natasha paused. "About my weakness."

For once, Mona felt Natasha was being sincere. "What happened when Rusty was murdered?"

"I honestly don't know. I was watching the race and heard Mrs. Thompson screaming. I turned and saw Mr. and Mrs. Duff standing over Rusty trying to help. I still didn't know what had happened because they were blocking the view of the body. It wasn't until Mr. Duff began yelling for the police that I realized something horrible had happened. Initially, I thought Rusty had a heart attack."

"If you told the Duffs about Rusty, why did you bring him to the Derby?"

"Because I never did. You said that I did, but I didn't."

"The Duffs said that you did."

"I didn't. It would have made my position weaker with Cody."

"Why didn't you and the Thompsons join the Duffs in Louisville the night before?"

"I don't know what you're talking about. The six of us hired a limo and came together from Lexington."

"You and the Duffs traveled from Lexington on the day of the Derby?"

"Yes, all four couples."

Mona hid her surprise that the Duffs had lied

to her. "What did you talk about?"

"Mostly chit chat, but it seemed Mr. Duff and Rusty were Civil War buffs. Rusty was telling about his grandfather's Confederate exploits. Apparently his old man kept a detailed diary about the war, and Mr. Duff spoke about his collection. They had lots to talk about."

"What about the war?"

"Mr. Duff was interested in Rusty's grandfather and offered to purchase the diary, but Rusty refused. Said it was a family heirloom."

"Was Mr. Duff angry?"

"Not at all."

"Did anyone change their seats in the box before the race?"

"Well, Helen, had a hissy fit when she learned that Cody and I were purchasing a horse together and stormed out of the box. She wasn't there for the race."

"You and the Thompsons arrived at the box later than the Duffs."

"Mrs. Thompson and I had to use the facilities first."

"Not Mrs. Duff or Helen?"

"No. They were fine or so they said."

"When did Helen learn of your partnership with Cody?"

"Cody mentioned it in the limo right before we arrived at Churchill Downs. He thought Helen would be pleased. She was not, and was steadily building up steam about it until she exploded in the private box."

"Were people switching seats in the viewing box?"

"Helen had been between Mrs. Duff and Cody. When she left, Cody moved next to his mother."

"So it was Mrs. Duff against the railing, Cody, empty seat, empty seat, Mr. Duff, empty seat on the aisle."

"Yes, I think so."

"Why are you so interested in Cody?"

"I'm interested in Cody's money—not him."

"Does he know that?"

"You flatter me, Mona. A woman of my age with that young man," Natasha scoffed.

"Everyone thinks the two of you are having an affair. It's making his wife miserable."

"She's Cody's problem. I have nothing to do with her."

"One more question—what does Alice Roosevelt have against you?"

"I may be hands off with Cody Duff, but that wasn't always the case. Let's just say I beat Alice at her own game. Now, if you would excuse me, I'll be going." Natasha gathered her purse and wrapped her fox stole around her shoulders before fleeing the ice cream parlor.

Mona watched Natasha cross the street and meet up with Giunto and Lolordo. How awful it must be for Natasha to be under their thumb. She wondered about the vig on the loan as she pulled out her wallet and put a dollar tip on the table. It must be exorbitant.

One of the soda jerks cleaned her table and swiped up the dollar bill. "Anything else, Miss?"

Mona looked out the front window and saw Jamison patiently keeping an eye on Giunto and Lolordo across the street. They, in turn, were watching him. Finally, the two mobsters melted into the crowd walking the street while Natasha went into a woman's dress store.

"Yes. I would like a strawberry milkshake, please. Can you make that to go?"

"Yes'am."

ABIGAIL KEAM

There were other questions to be answered. Did Natasha suggest Rusty as the mob's enforcer? If yes, was it because she knew of Rusty's reputation for cutting corners or that he was not averse to skimming off the top? Were the Duffs deliberately targeted by Natasha? Natasha was old money. The Duffs were new money. Old money always scorned new money, so why did Natasha make friends with them? And why cozy up to Cody? Did Natasha think she could worm her way into Cody's affections and then ask for money to pay off her debt with the Chicago boys?

While waiting for the milkshake for Jamison, Mona pondered about Natasha. What parts of her story could Mona believe and what was pure trash? That's what Mona needed to decipher.

Mona decided to pay another visit to Miss Alice.

22

Mona waited in the hotel lobby. Giunto and Lolordo's faces drained of color when they saw her sitting in a chair near a potted elephant ear plant. They whispered to each other before running up the stairs to their rooms. Within twenty minutes they checked out and caught a cab to the train depot. They were sure Mona was in the lobby to identify them to a G-man.

Mona wondered where the two had been, but she would get a report later, as she had them followed.

Natasha swept through the hotel door fifteen minutes later and caught the elevator. She didn't notice Mona.

A few minutes later, Alice made an entrance with reporters following her. "I'm just a regular citizen, fellows. I am not going to criticize the President publicly, but of course, privately, that is a different matter," she said, winking.

"Does that mean you don't approve of FDR's recovery policies?" one reported asked, with pencil to his pad.

Alice stopped, pointing at the young reporter. "Don't you dare print that, young man. I said no such thing."

"How do you get along with Mrs. Roosevelt?" another reporter asked.

"Cousin Eleanor? I refuse any of her invitations where mustard or ketchup are to be the main vegetables. Imagine—grilled hamburgers being cooked and served on the White House lawn. I know she's trying to be one of the people, but she's the First Lady. She's supposed to set standards. Not be one of the great unwashed."

"Now that you are a widow, what are your plans, Mrs. Longworth?"

"I have a simple motto for life, boys. Fill what's empty. Empty what's full. And scratch where it itches."

The reporters wrote feverishly on their tablets.

"Now you must excuse me. I have to dress.

I'm having dinner with the Governor and his wife." As Alice made her way through, she spied Mona and went over to her. "Mona, why are you sitting in this drab lobby?"

"Waiting for you, actually." As a newspaper photographer took a picture of them, Mona became momentarily blinded by the flash.

Alice threatened, "No more, boys. Take one more picture, and I'll not say another word for your newspapers. Your editors won't like that. This is a private conversation, so as they say in the South—GIT!"

The men twittered and moaned, but moved away from Alice. They knew she was notoriously flippant and might readily agree to talk with them again after conversing with Mona Moon, which in itself was news. Whatever Alice Longworth did or said made great copy.

Ignoring the reporters, Alice said, "Mona, let's go to my suite. These jackals won't let us have a moment's peace until we're out of sight."

As soon as Alice and Mona entered the elevator, the newsmen rushed over to the front desk trying to get Alice Roosevelt's room number from the desk clerks or the bellhops. Usually, the hotel employees were not averse to sliding an extra dollar or two in their pockets, but even a ten-dollar bill would not induce the hotel employees to betray Alice. She was too formidable a person to annoy, and they didn't want to lose their jobs.

As for Mona, she remained quiet until she reached Alice's penthouse suite.

Alice threw her coat and purse on a chair before taking off her hat so she could check her hair in a hall mirror. "Feel free to help yourself, Mona. The bourbon is over there," Alice said, pointing to a bar.

"I'll just take a Coca Cola," Mona said, putting some ice in a glass.

Satisfied that her hair was not mussed, Alice said, "Pour me one, too, with a little rum in it." She plopped down on the couch. "Thank you, dear," she said to Mona, who handed her a glass. "Oh, gawd, what a day I've had!" She held up her glass in salute. "Bottoms up."

Mona took a long swallow. "Didn't realize how thirsty I was. That tastes good." She took another sip.

"Why didn't you have the manager let you in

my suite instead of waiting in the lobby, Mona?"

"It seemed like an intrusion."

"May I ask why you needed to see me so urgently?"

"I wanted to ask you about Natasha Merriweather."

"Oh, her. What a relief. I thought you were going to try to get me to wrangle you an invitation to the White House. I don't understand this country's fascination with Saint Eleanor. We're first cousins, you know. My father was her uncle."

"Yes, I'm aware."

"We grew up together, but that's where it ends. Even as children, Eleanor was a goody two-shoes. Positively repulsive. She acts so pure she must fart gladiolas."

"I understand you two were close at one time."

"That's true, somewhat. My mother died when I was very young, and Eleanor's mother wanted very little to do with her as a small child. Her mother was very beautiful and disappointed that Eleanor looked—well, like Eleanor—so plain. Then, like my mother, she died young.

Eleanor and I were cast adrift together for months at a time at our Aunt Anna's home. My father was consumed with work, and her father was preoccupied as well. They couldn't spare the time to care for us."

"I understand Eleanor's father died at thirty-four from a seizure."

"That's putting perfume on a skunk. Uncle Elliott died a drunk. It's the truth of the matter. As we matured into adults, Eleanor and I grew apart. In the end, Eleanor's a Hyde Park Roosevelt and I'm an Oyster Bay Roosevelt. We both have different outlooks on life. She wants to save the world, and I would like another rum and coke." Alice held out her empty glass to Mona.

As fascinating as this conversation was, Mona came for a different reason, but she couldn't help but recall the rumor that the feud between the two women began when Franklin Roosevelt became besotted with plain Eleanor and not the fabulous Alice. If true, it must have damaged Alice's pride immensely. Mona took Alice's empty glass and placed it on an end table. "Alice, I need you to focus. What is between you and Natasha Merriweather?"

Alice raised an eyebrow. "Why do you want to know?"

"Because Natasha lured me into an alley to meet two goons from Chicago this afternoon. She says it was to extract information, but I think it was to smash my head in. It seems the Chicago Outfit knows who I am and is interested in what I do. I don't like that. I think their interest revolves around Rusty Thompson's death, but I'm not positive. It may have something to do with you."

"My relationship with Natasha has nothing to do with Rusty Thompson or the mob from Chicago I can assure you."

"I want the reason."

Seeing Mona was determined, Alice said, "Very well. She was a *friend* of my husband."

"Oh." Mona felt her cheeks grow hot. She knew of Nicholas Longworth's reputation as a skirt chaser.

"Yes, oh. It happened a long time ago, but I've never forgiven her. I knew Nicholas had affairs. I just thought he wouldn't sleep with someone from our social circle."

"I'm sorry."

"No need for you to be sorry. Natasha and I haven't spoken to each other in years."

"I'm surprised she had the nerve to come to the garden party."

"And pass a chance to rub my nose in it again?" Alice shook her head. "It doesn't really matter anymore. Nicholas is dead and doesn't concern my life now. It's all in the past. Best forgotten."

"She's staying at the hotel. It must make you feel uncomfortable."

"Natasha moved out. She's living at Pennygate Farm now. Frances Dodge ran into her several days ago and gave me the lowdown."

"I just saw her enter the lobby and go upstairs."

"She might be going to Cody's room."

"Doesn't it bother you that Natasha might have had something to do with Rusty Thompson's death?"

"Oh, my dear, Mona. She had nothing to do with Mr. Thompson's death."

Mona asked, "How do you know that?"

"Because I saw who killed Rusty Thompson, and it was not Natasha!"

23

"YOU WHAT!" Mona gasped.

"I saw who killed Rusty Thompson."

"Why didn't you say anything?"

"And get involved in a tacky murder. I should say not."

"You let the police humiliate Willie Deatherage in front of all those people when you knew she was innocent."

"Most unfortunate. I rather like her." Alice looked closely at Mona's furious expression. "I knew she would be set free—eventually."

"That's why you were so eager to help Willie at the garden party. You felt guilty."

"Guilty? Me? Heaven's no," Alice laughed. "I helped Mrs. Deatherage because I know what it is to be bullied. My father bullied me. 'Alice, do this. Alice, be more like your brothers. Alice, why can't you be more circumspect like Cousin Eleanor?'"

"Alice, can we concentrate on Rusty Thompson?" Mona was growing tired of Alice's self-centeredness. "Are you going to tell me who did it?"

"No."

"NO!"

"No."

"It's your duty to come forward."

"Let me tell you what would happen if I did so. It would become a three-ring circus. The murderer would probably get off because he would not be able to get a fair trial. Politics would seep into the proceedings and taint the entire process. It would cease to be about justice and more about what I was wearing at the trial and what quips I might say." Alice leaned forward toward Mona. "I know you think I'm horrid for keeping it to myself, but I am experienced in these matters. My coming forward will only make matters worse. If this person is to be caught, it must be without my assistance."

"If that is so, then why confide in me?"

Alice chuckled. "I don't want to see the culprit get away with this murder any more than you do. I've been pushing you in the right direction. All you have to do is follow the clues."

"Why me? Why not the police?"

"Detective McCaw was correct when he insisted coming to the garden party. He knew the murderer was to be found in Lexington and not Louisville. He just couldn't connect the dots because he didn't have all the facts. But you, my dear, have no such restraints as the police. Besides that, you are a natural born snoop. You like solving riddles. It is in your nature. That's why I've stayed. I wanted to see if you are as smart as you think you are."

Mona was exasperated. "I don't know quite what to say. I feel quite put upon, Alice. I don't think I've ever met anyone as calculating as you."

"I think your Aunt Melanie might put me to shame. I recognized her as a kindred soul right off. Better watch your back with her."

"You really are not going to tell who murdered Rusty Thompson?"

"I'm not."

"Since you've been using the pronoun "he," I

can assume the murderer is male."

"Not necessarily."

"Female?"

"Follow the clues, Mona. The answer is right in front of you. You just don't know that you know."

"Is there anything else you might tell me?"

"I've told you all that I can. I wish you the best in this matter."

"How long are you staying?"

"Until the end of next week. I'll be going to Cincinnati to see old friends. After that, I will be in New York before heading to the Adirondacks for the summer. I hope you catch your 'man' before I leave."

Mona stood. "I guess there is nothing left to say."

"I guess not, but you might get me another rum and coke before you leave."

"Unbelievable," Mona muttered, before storming out of the suite. She had never met a more selfish person in her life. Mona paused. That was not true. She had encountered more ruthless and dangerous people, but never as spoiled and entitled as Alice Longworth. Mona suddenly felt sorry for Alice as she remembered her own mother's love and tenderness. Perhaps it was the lack of a mother's guidance that made Alice into the woman she was. Mona guessed Alice had to be a tough cookie growing up in Teddy Roosevelt's household. In the hallway, she glanced at her watch. Oh, dear. She was going to be late, and this was a formal dinner night. Monsieur Bisaillon would be furious if his meal was served later than usual.

Mona was hurrying to catch the elevator when she spied a small black man in a white jacket emptying the hall ashtrays. Oh well, she was sure Monsieur Bisaillon would get over his anger as she was going to be tardy—again.

24

Back at home, Mona held up her gold lamé evening gown as she ran down the staircase. One of her shoe straps came undone, so Mona stopped on a stair, removed her shoes, and continued down with the shoes in her hands.

Samuel met her at the bottom.

"What did you tell him?"

"As far as Bisaillon thinks, you are in the dining room enjoying the second course."

"Thanks for covering for me, Samuel."

"It's a pleasure. Anything to keep peace in the kitchen."

"Is Lord Farley here?"

"He started without you, Miss Mona."

"Excellent." Mona entered the dining room, pausing to slip on her shoes.

Lord Farley stood until Mona was seated. "I was beginning to get worried."

"I'm so sorry that I'm late. It's been a frightful day, Robert. My head is still reeling."

Robert picked up his water glass. "Would you like a sympathetic ear?"

Mona waited until Samuel had left the room. "Alice Longworth told me she witnessed the murder."

Robert's eyes widened. "That's quite a confession. Why hasn't she told the police?"

"Alice said it would create havoc instead of helping."

"I think she's right, darling."

Mona sighed. "I wasn't thinking of that possibility. I was concentrating on what Willie and Dexter were put through."

"Who did it?"

"She wouldn't tell me."

"That's not quite hunky-dory. Have you a clue?"

"She said I knew without knowing it."

Robert cut into his fish. "I'm sure you'll figure it out. You always do."

"Aren't you curious?"

"I'm consumed with getting our wedding back on track. I wish you'd pay more attention to our intended nuptials, Mona."

"What news do you have on that front?"

"Father's conceded to us visiting this summer."

Mona smiled. "That's good news, isn't it? Why look so gloomy?"

"Father can be a right-old buzzard. I think he means to make mincemeat out of you."

"Robert, it will be all right. You go ahead and purchase the tickets. I'll have Violet stitch me up some smart outfits, and I'll put on the dog for your relatives. Your father won't have a chance to disapprove of me. Speaking of dogs, have you seen Chloe?"

"She's under the table sulking. I wouldn't give her any food from the table."

Mona leaned down and peeked under the table cloth. "Poor baby. Chloe, don't be mad. I'll give you a treat after dinner. I just don't want you begging while we're eating. Be a good girl, now. Come on. That's it. Here's a nice pet to tie you over until you get your treat." Mona scratched Chloe behind the ears as the dog lay her head in

Mona's lap. Mona rang the silver dinner bell.

Samuel entered the dining room. "Yes, Miss Mona."

"Can you take Chloe, please? This food is too much of a temptation."

"That's where she's been hiding. I've been looking all over for her. Come on, dog."

Chloe followed Samuel out of the room wagging her tail.

Mona said, "Where were we?"

"You said to purchase the tickets. How many?"

Mona thought for a moment. "I want Violet and Dotty to go with me, I guess three on my side. What about you?"

"I'll just need one."

"Won't you need a valet? Who will dress you?"

Robert grinned. "I know how to dress myself, Mona. You've watched me."

Mona chuckled. "I mean it's customary for a lord to have a male attendant. We don't want your father to think you are slipping. Standards must be kept up."

"My father has plenty of servants that can

pinch hit as a valet. No need to worry."

Mona pulled her roll apart and buttered a piece. "I'll clear my schedule with Dexter and get back to you on dates."

"Very good." Robert took a bite of his salmon. "This is very good. Steamed?"

"Poached, I believe."

"I like the sauce."

"The lemon and capers bring out the subtleness of the fish. Goes well with it."

"Is that why you were late?"

"Meeting with Alice? No. When I was leaving, I ran into Jellybean Martin. He and I talked for a lengthy bit of time, and he let me in the room of the two men who attacked me this afternoon. He had a master key."

"I was wondering when you were going to broach the subject."

"I knew as soon as Dexter knew, he would phone you."

"It was all I could do not to jump into a car and find those men. Give them a good pummeling."

"I understand Dexter called the FBI."

"He did."

"I saw the men check out of the hotel. I'm sure they were on the next train out of town. I haven't seen the report on them yet."

"It's on your desk."

"Have you read it?"

"It said they left on the five o'clock train to Cincinnati. Your men are following them now."

"Good riddance. Lexington doesn't need trash like them."

"Did you find anything in their rooms?"

"Some disgusting pictures. You know what I mean."

"I do."

"Other than empty cheap whiskey bottles and piles of dirty towels, not much. Jellybean helped me turn over the mattresses and look behind wall pictures."

"Did you look behind drawers?"

"We did, but nothing."

"It's a wonder Jellybean didn't blow his cover."

"He told me the hotel management was so impressed that they hired him full time as an undercover shamus. He apparently discovered it was hotel staff who was pilfering."

"That's good. Is he going to take the job?"

"He's considering it. Jellybean thinks he might be able to offer his services to guests who get into a jam while visiting our fair city."

"That man is always thinking about an angle."

"He needs the money. Why shouldn't Jellybean take advantage of the situation and work on the side? Black folk are hard pressed in this economy."

"Not going to argue with you on the subject of Jellybean. Changing the direction of this conversation, I understand Jamison was magnificent."

"He certainly was, with the help of his sawed-off shotgun. I'm going to have to do something especially nice for him."

"Speaking of protection, we are going to have to include bodyguards on our trip, Mona."

"I know, but can we discuss it later?"

"Yes, but security needs to be addressed."

"I will see to it. Don't badger me about it now, please."

"You want to talk about Rusty Thompson?"

"I do. Ever since Elspeth Hopper got away with murdering her half-sister, it's been sticking in my craw. I don't intend for this murderer to get off as well."

"What are you going to do, darling?"

"Find the murderer, of course, and I'll do it before I get on that boat to England."

"Hear. Hear. As Teddy Roosevelt would say, 'BULLY.' You have the stuff of a duchess, Mona."

Mona blushed even though she loved it when Robert praised her. They remained quiet, each in their own thoughts.

Robert was thinking of things he needed to do before they left for England, while Mona mused over what Alice had told her. She knew, but she didn't know that she knew. That's what Alice had said. After dinner, Mona was going to write down the events on Derby day, step by step, and every conversation she had with the Duffs and Merri-weathers since then. Somewhere in her ruminating, she would stumble across the why, the how, and the who of Rusty Thompson's murder.

25

Five days later, Natasha looked about Mona's drawing room. In various chairs and couches sat Zeke and Jeannie Duff, Cody and Helen Duff, Willie and Dexter Deatherage, Alice Longworth, and Robert Farley.

Melanie Moon followed Natasha into the room, whereupon Alice patted the seat next to her on the couch and said, "Melanie, you haven't got anything nice to say about anybody, so come sit next to me."

"What is this?" Natasha asked, taken aback, seeing everyone.

"May I get you a drink?" Robert offered. "This is going to take a while."

Mona entered the room last and shut the door. "I thought it was time for all of us to have a little chat about Rusty Thompson's death."

Natasha shot back, "Why isn't Mrs. Thompson here?"

"She's not needed for our talk, but she might speak for the prosecution if my guess is correct."

Natasha hissed, "You're wasting everyone's morning on a guess! You must think mightily of yourself to squander our time so."

"Sit down, Natasha," Alice said. "I want to hear what Mona has to say."

"So do I for once," concurred Melanie.

"Thank you, Alice and Aunt Melanie." Mona said, taking center stage.

Natasha sat down in a huff next to Melanie, who smiled greedily at her. Melanie liked watching people squirm. The others gave Mona their undivided attention.

"I want to thank you all for coming on short notice, but I didn't have all the information until last night," Mona said, holding up a file box.

"I thought I was coming for a brunch," Mrs. Duff said.

"A luncheon will be served after my presentation, Mrs. Duff, but not everyone will be in the mood to eat."

"What does she mean?" Jeannie Duff asked her husband, who looked about perplexed. Zeke Duff was as confused as his wife.

Mona said, "Fruit and little cakes are placed on the side tables to nibble on while I'm talking. Please help yourselves."

Melanie grabbed a tiny blueberry muffin and stuffed it in her mouth before saying, "Get on with it, Mona."

"Be patient, Melanie. I'm getting there." Mona tugged on her navy suit jacket. "Since the awful day at the Derby when Rusty Thompson was murdered with Wilhelmina's hat pin, there has been a cornucopia of misdirection."

"In other words, we've all been lying," Alice said, looking about the room.

"Almost everyone. A few have been telling the truth. Aunt Melanie is one and the Deatherages are the other two."

Robert chuckled, "Your Uncle Manfred must be rolling in his grave at that twist, Melanie. You telling the truth for once."

"Oh, shut up, Robert," Melanie shot back.

"I hope you are not implying that we have lied," Mrs. Duff protested.

"Yes, I am."

"I'm not going to sit here and be insulted," Mr. Duff said, rising. "Come, dear."

"Mr. Duff, please sit down. You won't be allowed to leave. I have the house surrounded by my men and all the doors are locked."

"This is outrageous!" Mr. Duff yelled.

"I agree. It is outrageous, but so is murder. Sit down, Mr. Duff and behave," Mona said.

Melanie laughed at Mr. Duff's blustering expression until she realized she was locked in also. "Hurry this up. I have a hair appointment."

"You always have a hair appointment. Makes me wonder why you're not bald," Mona mumbled.

Alice snickered until Melanie turned around and pinched her.

A chalkboard had been placed in front of the fireplace. Mona picked up a stick of chalk and quickly made a diagram. "As you can see, I have drawn our boxes which were next to each other. Did I place everyone in the correct seat at the time of the murder?"

Helen spoke up. "I left before the race had started."

Mona took a wet cloth and erased Helen's name. "Where did you go, Helen?"

"I went to the ladies room and then to the bar for a drink."

"Did you come back out again?"

"Yes, at the very end of the race, but I was far away from our box."

"That's not completely true," Melanie said. "Before the race, I was scanning the crowd and saw you standing in the aisle behind Rusty Thompson, and you were shooting daggers at him. You were wearing that god-awful orange dress so you stood out. With your orange fascinator as well, you looked like a pumpkin."

Mona frowned at Melanie. "Let's keep this somewhat civil, Aunt Melanie."

Not cowered by Melanie's remarks, Helen said, "I usually kill rattlesnakes. Never come across one that stood on two legs, though." She pleaded her case to the group. "I was standing behind Mr. Thompson and went back inside to the bar. When I heard the race was about to start, I came back out and stood on the stairs above our box so I could see. If I was standing on the stairs, I could have hardly killed Mr. Thompson and then rush through that crowd back to the staircase. You saw how packed it was."

"But you pushed through the crowd for the ladies room and the bar," Mona said.

"I left before the race. People were still mingling. The aisles were not jammed."

"I understand you don't like Kentucky," Mona stated.

"I prefer Texas. I don't care for the Thoroughbred business. We have horses in Texas."

"Texas horses are good for rodeos and barrel racing. You have to come to Kentucky if you want to race in the sport of kings. You have to be where the king makers are," Cody said.

"I think this racing venture is nonsense and a waste of money," Helen said, flashing a look of contempt at Natasha.

"Is that what you two fought about at the Derby?" Mona asked.

"Yes," Helen said, casting down her eyes. "Among other things."

Alice asked, "What other things?"

"Personal."

"They will just make you testify in court what the argument was about," Alice said. "Your dislike of the racing industry gives you a motive for killing Thompson. It would have been easy for you to pick up Willie's hat pin off the floor, stand behind Rusty Thompson, and, during the race, pat him on the back. When he turned, you pushed the hat pin into his eye."

Helen jumped up. "NO! You can't be serious! I didn't even know the man except to say hello."

Mona tossed the chalk at Helen which she caught with her left hand. "You're left-handed."

"Yes," Helen said, a little dazed.

"Sit down, girl," Alice said. "Miss Mona just proved you didn't kill Mr. Thompson."

"What?" she mumbled while accepting a glass of water from Robert.

"We are looking for a right-handed person," Mona said.

Cody put his arm around his wife. "You knew she didn't kill Thompson, and yet you put her through this nightmare of questioning. I object to your methods, Miss Moon."

Undeterred, Mona asked, "Did you move your seat at all before the race, Cody?"

Mrs. Duff fluttered her hands. "You are going too far. Why are you picking on us? It was probably his wife who killed Thompson. She was sitting next to him."

"Be quiet, Mother," Cody said. "I'll answer Miss Moon's question. The sooner we clear up that we had nothing to do with the murder, the sooner we can get out of here."

"I'm waiting," Mona said.

"After Helen left, I moved into her seat next to Mother."

"Helen, may I have the chalk? Thank you." Mona indicated the change on the blackboard. "It is now Mrs. Duff sitting against the railing, Cody, empty seat, empty seat, Mr. Duff, empty seat."

"That's correct," Mr. Duff said.

"Cody, your wife says the quarrel in the private box is personal, yet we could hear Helen arguing with you from our box. Arguing in public is no longer a private affair. It is gist for the gossip mongers. Clear up the matter of the argument and tell us what it was about."

"Natasha let it slip we had purchased a horse together and that I was underwriting its training and vet care."

"Natasha said it was you who let it slip about your partnership in the limo right before Churchill Downs."

ABIGAIL KEAM

"Did I? Maybe. I thought Helen knew," Natasha said.

"I don't really remember," Cody said.

"Are you underwriting all of this horse's care?" Robert asked.

"Natasha is boarding it."

"Boarding a horse is cheap next to the training and vet costs. Who pays the employees like exercise riders, jockeys, hot walkers, not to mention the equipment? Saddles and tack are not cheap," Robert said.

"I do."

Robert asked, "How are the profits to be shared?"

Cody said, "Fifty-fifty."

Robert couldn't believe the boy's naivety. "Natasha gets fifty percent of a winning purse while you have put up ninety percent of the horse's upkeep. That's not an advantageous deal for you."

"That's what I've been trying to tell Cody," Helen said, looking vindicated.

"I'm teaching him the ropes," Natasha insisted. "Introducing him to important people in the racing business. I'm giving him my time."

Both Alice and Melanie twittered.

"What's so funny?" Natasha said, shooting both women a hateful look.

"Was this okay with you, Mr. Duff?" Robert asked.

"Cody didn't ask for my counsel, Lord Farley. I didn't know all the aspects of their arrangement. He told me the basics and that's all." Mr. Duff turned to Natasha. "You took advantage of my son."

"I did no such thing," Natasha objected.

Mona said, "Cody, you should know the only reason Natasha has any interest in you is due to your money. She is a gambler and needed an infusion of cash. She also has ties to the Chicago Outfit, Capone's old gang."

Jeannie Duff gasped.

"That's ridiculous. Her family has one of the largest fortunes in the country," Cody said.

"I'm sorry, young man," Dexter said, "but I've had Natasha checked out. It's true she bought Pennygate Farm, but it is in her father's name. In fact, Natasha Merriweather owns nothing outright. Her father owns everything and does so because he is aware of his daughter's financial instability. That's why she needed you."

Cody looked crushed and asked Natasha, "Was everything you said to me a lie?"

Natasha looked away. "Mr. Deatherage is telling the truth. I was only interested in the money. Doesn't mean I'm not fond of you, Cody, but it ends there."

Flummoxed, Cody turned away and discreetly wiped his eyes.

Helen clasped her hands in her lap. The truth of Cody and Natasha's relationship was out in the open at last. She gave a sigh of relief.

Everyone remained quiet for a few seconds. Even Alice looked at the boy in pity.

"Where's your husband, Mrs. Merriweather?" Willie asked.

"I guess there is no point in concealing the truth. He thought what I was doing was disgraceful, so he left me. He hasn't a penny to his name, but Mr. Merriweather left me, an heiress, on principle." Natasha laughed bitterly.

"I want to get back to the main subject at hand," Mona said, looking at Cody and Helen. "What was your connection to Rusty Thompson?"

Helen said, "I already told you. We didn't have one, really. We knew him through Natasha. She recommended him as a trainer."

"Did you hire him, Cody?"

"I was considering it, but Father said he was iffy, so I put him out of the running, so to speak."

"Why were the Thompsons invited to the private viewing box?"

Cody answered, "I don't know, Miss Moon. I thought they were guests of Natasha's."

"Did you also think the Thompsons had been invited by Natasha, Mr. Duff?"

"Yes."

Mona opened her file and pulled out a hand-written note. "Do you remember this, Mrs. Duff?"

Mrs. Duff's eyes widened when she saw the stationery. "I'm not sure that I do."

"It is the Phoenix Hotel's official stationery. You can see their logo and address on it." Mona held up the note for all to see. "It is a note inviting the Thompsons to the Derby. It's signed by you." She handed the note to Mrs. Duff.

"I may have invited them before we knew of

Rusty's reputation. I don't remember."

"Look at the date in the upper right-hand corner. It was written only four days before the Kentucky Derby took place."

Mrs. Duff looked at her husband for guidance.

"You forget, Mrs. Duff, when I had a drink with you in the bar at the Phoenix Hotel, you said the Merriweathers had invited the Thompsons and you were surprised to see them."

"I must have forgotten. So much has been happening."

Mona said, "It's come down to this. There were only seven people in your box at the time of the murder. Helen had left. One of you did it. It had to be one of you."

"Preposterous," Mr. Duff blustered. "It could have been anyone standing in the aisle or behind Thompson."

"I'm going to come back to that, but first I want to discuss the shooting at the garden party."

Natasha groaned.

Mona smiled. "Yes, Natasha, it comes back to you again."

"I never thought Mrs. Thompson would go as

far as getting a gun and shooting up the place."

"Yes, you did. You knew Rusty had a gun because he told you he bought one. It only makes sense after the debacle with Ed Bradley. He knew there would be payback from the Chicago Outfit. What he didn't know was that you were working for the mob and feeding them information, originally pointing him out to them as a patsy. You fingered him. Once they knew of his slightly shady ethics, the mob had their hooks in Thompson, and all the time, you sat back and watched it happen."

Alice tsk tsked. "Natasha, you've been a naughty girl."

Mr. Duff pointed a finger at Natasha. "She must have done it. Everything points to her."

Mona continued, "Natasha, you went to the Thompson house several hours before the party. Mrs. Thompson thought you were checking on her, but you were really 'checking up on her.' She was having a cup of coffee, and you asked for one as well. When Mrs. Thompson had her back turned, you slipped something into her cup and then proceeded to get her 'riled up' as they say here. You planted the seed of her getting her husband's gun and exacting revenge at the party."

"What did you put in the woman's coffee, Natasha?" Alice asked.

Natasha lowered her head in shame. "A cocktail of cocaine and a crushed mushroom that contained psilocybin."

Robert gasped, "Psilocybin is a hallucinogenic alkaloid!"

"It's a wonder the poor woman regained her mind. You must have been mad to give Mrs. Thompson something like that," Dexter admonished. His stomach lurched and he needed a bicarbonate—and a shower. There was too much filth in the room.

"I told you Natasha did it. Everything points to her," Mr. Duff accused. "I insist you call the police."

"She will be arrested for the poisoning of Mrs. Thompson and her part in the attack of Ed Bradley's horse, Bazaar." Mona stared at Natasha. "The attack was for the horse and not Mr. Bradley I assume."

Natasha nodded. "Bradley had won the last two Derbys. The mob couldn't afford for him to win again. The mob was placing bets on Mata

Hari to show, as they didn't think she could win."

"Why not?" Willie asked.

"Because she's a filly," Natasha said. "Fillies don't win the Kentucky Derby as they are not as big as the stallions. As you saw, she didn't even show. She came in fourth. The mob lost their money."

Mona asked, "What about the other strong contenders?"

"Bradley put out the word on what had happened, and the other owners beefed up their security."

"So the mob killed Mr. Thompson?" Willie asked. "I'm getting confused."

"Everything points to them," Robert said, perplexed. "It doesn't matter if Natasha was the killer. They gave the order."

"Natasha was sitting seven seats from Rusty. She would have had to step in front of her husband, two empty seats, and Mrs. Thompson to get to Rusty. Mrs. Thompson said no one exchanged seats on their row during the race," Mona explained.

"I couldn't have done it," Natasha said. "Alice, even you must see my killing Thompson was impossible."

"I'm withholding judgment," Alice replied.

"What are we waiting for?" Mr. Duff pleaded. "Natasha killed Thompson. Surely, everyone can see it."

"Natasha didn't kill Thompson," Mona said, looking in her file box.

"How can you say that after all we've heard?" Mr. Duff asked, reaching for his wife's hand.

Mona glanced up. "For one simple reason, Mr. Duff. You killed Rusty Thompson!"

26

Mr. Duff rose from the couch. "I'll be taking my leave now."

"As I said, no one is permitted to leave."

"You can't keep people against their will, Miss Moon. Come on, Jeannie. We're going."

"Mr. Duff, there is an eyewitness to the murder. Someone in this room saw you do it. There's no getting around it."

"Who? Who makes such a claim?"

"They wish to remain anonymous for the time being, but they are prepared to testify in court."

Frantically looking between her husband and Mona, Mrs. Duff said, "There is no way my husband could do such a thing."

Cody jumped in to defend his father. "How could he have possibly done so in front of all those people?"

"But he did and was seen doing so."

"Why hasn't this witness come forth before now?" Cody asked. "You're making this up."

"I'm afraid not."

"Then how did I do it?" Mr. Duff asked.

"It wasn't premeditated, but your hate being so strong, you acted without thinking of the consequences. I think you saw Mrs. Deatherage's fallen hat pin on the ground and picked it up. You waited until everyone was enthralled with the race, scooted over until you were facing Rusty Thompson, who was also standing and cheering on the race. You leaned toward him as though you were going to speak, and using your hat to shield your hand, stabbed him in the eye and simply turned around cheering on the race. Thompson collapsed into his chair and died without anyone the wiser. It was quiet, fast, and efficient."

"I had no motive to kill him."

"You did. A very strong one. Revenge. The sins of the father visited upon the child."

"Revenge for what?" Mrs. Duff asked. "We didn't know the man, but for a couple of months."

"Mrs. Thompson gave me permission to look through her husband's things. I was particularly interested in his Civil War collection. I found a diary maintained by a Private Jarrod Thompson, his grandfather." Mona pulled a weather beaten and scarred leather diary from the box. "Jarrod Thompson was a sixteen-year-old boy who, against his mother's advice, ran off to join the Confederate cause. He thought the war would be a glorious affair with melodious trumpets, grand cavalry charges, and uniforms with shiny brass buttons. He imagined himself to be a conquering hero winning all sorts of medals. Instead, Jarrod found himself confronting the terror of war— starvation, filth, illness, maimed bodies, and death. He came to find that he didn't like military life and didn't care about the Confederate dream any longer. Jarrod just wanted out and to get as far from the killing and dying as he could. It was during the battle at Perryville, Kentucky in October of 1862, when Jarrod and a few compadres decided to desert and travel to St. Louis from where they would venture into the West and make their fortunes." Mona paused.

"Go on," Mr. Duff whispered.

"Jarrod and his companions got lost. They crossed the Ohio River instead of the Mississippi River as they had no map nor a compass between them. They came upon a farm near the banks of the Ohio, where lived a family comprised of a man and a woman with a small boy."

Mr. Duff put his head in his hands and swayed.

"The next four days are missing from the diary. On the fifth day, Jarrod writes that the farmer had been belligerent to the soldiers, so they killed him in retribution. The woman and the boy were left for dead after four days of abuse." Mona closed the diary. "I can only imagine what your grandmother and father went through those four days."

"My granny told me before she died. It was horrific."

"Did your father lose an eye during those four days, Mr. Duff?"

Mr. Duff refused to raise his head. "One of the men gouged out his eye because my father wasn't fast enough bringing him the whiskey jug."

Mona bowed her head, and the rest of the room was deadly quiet. "Sir, if it's any consolation to you, Jarrod Thompson never forgave himself for what happened to your family." She handed the diary to him. "If you read the last page, Jarrod details what he and the others did to your family. He regrets his actions and pleads for God to have mercy upon his soul."

"You think some squiggles on a page make up for what those savages did to my family."

"There were horrors committed on both sides, Mr. Duff," Alice said. "Union soldiers did dreadful things as well. Most of the country decided to put the war behind them and move forward."

"You weren't even born then. What would you know?"

"Neither were you. Let the dead bury the dead," Alice said. "The tragedy died with your father, and yet you brought it into the twentieth century—almost seventy years later. It must stop."

"When a young man, I promised my grandmother that I would look for those men and kill them for the deaths of our kin."

"The men responsible are all dead," Alice said, disgusted.

Duff replied, "Like you said, Miss Moon, the sins of the father are visited upon the child."

Mona took back the diary and placed it in the file box. "Mr. Duff, I'm so sorry."

"I'm not," Mr. Duff replied.

Robert picked up the phone and made a call. "Sheriff Monahan, please send out a car. Miss Moon has discovered the murderer of Rusty Thompson. You might want to inform Detective McCaw. Uh-huh. Yes. Yes. That's right. Come to Moon Manor. We'll be waiting. Thank you." Placing the receiver in the cradle, Robert turned to the group. "Sheriff Monahan is on his way."

Mona sat next to Robert, who took hold of her hand and squeezed reassuringly.

The rest of the room waited in silence for the cry of the police siren.

27

Violet picked up a piece of toast and slathered orange marmalade on it. "How did Mr. Duff know Rusty Thompson was the son of Jarrod Thompson? Thompson's a common name."

Mona put down her paper to answer Violet. "Duff's grandmother told him the names of the deserters and their hometowns. He had been searching for them a long time and had accumulated a great deal of information. It was one of the reasons Duff wanted to come to Kentucky. He was aware of Thompson. It would seem that Mr. Duff's suspicions about Rusty were confirmed during the ride to the Kentucky Derby. According to Mrs. Thompson, the two men had been discussing their Civil War collections, and Rusty mentioned his father's diary saying there had been some mishap at a farm in Illinois, but his father had never spoken about the incident. Rusty only learned of his father's war experiences after the old man had passed away, and Rusty discovered the diary hidden under some floorboards in his grandfather's bedroom."

"Rusty was a true innocent?"

"In this matter, yes."

"Why did Mr. and Mrs. Duff lie about staying in Louisville the night before the Derby?"

Mona replied, "They were throwing mud on the wall to see what stuck. They didn't want anyone to make a connection that Zeke and Rusty were both Civil War enthusiasts. It was the one thing connecting the two men and the motive for the murder. The Duffs knew Cody and Helen would back them up, and they paid off the driver of the limo for his silence. A good thing for us, the driver cooperated with the police when approached. With Mrs. Thompson and Mr. Merriweather conveniently leaving town, there was only Natasha to say otherwise. It's funny that Natasha unwittingly helped Duff conceal his crime by her criminal diversions. Duff must have loved it. Fortunately, the truth finally came out."

"Miss Mona, was there really a witness to the murder?"

Mona crossed her heart. "I cannot tell a lie. There was."

"Is that person going to come forward?"

"I doubt it. Altruism is not part of that person's makeup."

"I guess it was Mrs. Longworth then."

"I am neither confirming nor denying."

Violet sulked, "She told me I had buck teeth, and that I looked like a dazed bunny."

"Your teeth are fine. Mrs. Longworth likes to leave an impression with people by saying outrageous things."

"Do I have buck teeth?"

"Violet, you do not, and you don't look like a crazed rabbit either."

"Hurt my feelings."

"I can imagine."

Mona slid a gift box over to Violet. "This might make you feel better."

"What's this?"

"Open it."

Violet tore open the box and let out a huge woohoo when she saw a ticket for the ocean liner

Carinthia. "You're taking me with you to England again!"

"We'll leave from New York and arrive in Liverpool. I'll need several new outfits for the trip, Violet. You'll need to make several for yourself as well. We must put on the dog for these red coats."

"I have the patterns to several smart traveling suits."

"You have a month to prepare before we leave."

"Does this mean you are really going to marry Lord Farley?"

"It means we are visiting his father, but there shall be no talk of a wedding with the other employees here or across the pond."

"My lips are sealed. Oh, gosh, I'm so happy. I must hurry downtown. A new fabric store has opened. I know just the material for your wedding dress. I'll bring back a sample." Grabbing another piece of toast, Violet dashed off.

Chuckling, Mona picked up the morning paper again and perused the articles, but there was nothing amusing in the paper. The longshoremen strike on the West Coast still continued, closing down all the harbors in California, Oregon, and many in Washington. In Ohio, the American Federation of Labor was still striking against the Toledo Electric Auto-Life Co., and the situation was becoming more contentious every day. The article predicted more violence would ensue as the strike went on. Mona felt anger as she read about the strikes because they were so unnecessary. If the workers had been paid a decent wage, they would not be striking. Of course, the companies complained they couldn't pay more because of the Depression, and for some businesses, that may have been true, but not all.

Mona was determined that Moon Enterprises not suffer from strikes. She read the articles carefully and determined that money was not the only issue the workers were complaining about, but safer working conditions and health care as well. After she came back from Europe, Mona decided she would go out west to personally inspect the Moon mines. If there were grievances from the miners, she would deal with their complaints then. Otherwise, Dexter could handle the company until she returned.

She turned to the World News page. France

was still reeling from a pro-fascist riot in February when fifteen protesters were shot and killed by the police at the Place de la Concorde. In Germany, labor unions had been banned, and the Nazi Party had effectively taken over the German labor force.

Mona had come to agree with Robert that Adolph Hitler was more than just bluster. He and Mussolini, Prime Minister of Italy, were changing the democratic institutions of their countries and altering the face of Europe. The world was in upheaval, and events had been put into motion that would have far-reaching consequences, but to what end was anyone's guess.

Mona put down the paper wondering what she could do to help the world. It was true that she was rich. It was true she ran an important company and employed close to a thousand people. On the other hand, Mona lived in a backwater town, according to most people, and on a farm where the smell of horse manure often permeated the air. She had no connections in Washington and mostly irritated the local officials in her adopted state of Kentucky. Her one true gift was stumbling across dead bodies and figuring out who had murdered them.

Mr. Thomas entered the breakfast room. "Miss Mona, you have a telegram." He lowered a silver tray.

Curious, Mona picked up the Western Union envelope. "Thank you, Mr. Thomas. That is all." Quickly opening it, she read—

LUNCHEON INVITATION WITH ST. ELEANOR STOP MAY 30TH WHITEHOUSE 1 PM SHARP STOP BRING BUCK TOOTH BUNNY STOP BEST REGARDS ALICE

Albert Benjamin "Happy" Chandler Sr. (1898-1991)

Chandler was the 44th and 49th governor of Kentucky as well as a U.S. Senator with aspirations for becoming president. In 1982, he was inducted into the Baseball Hall of Fame for integrating baseball with Jackie Robinson when he was the Commissioner of Baseball (1945-1951).

Al Capone (1899-1947)

Capone was an American gangster sometimes known as Scarface. He rose to the leadership of the Chicago Outfit gang during the Prohibition era until he was indicted for tax fraud from evidence gathered by FBI agent Eliot Ness and the "Untouchables." He is thought to be behind the St. Valentine's Day Massacre of the rival North Side Gang and orders for thirty-three deaths throughout his criminal career.

Alice Blue

Alice blue is a pale shade of gray-blue associated with Alice Roosevelt Longworth as it was her signature color. The song, *Alice Blue Gown*, premiered in the 1919 Broadway musical *Irene*.

The color is used by the United States Navy for the insignia and trim on the USS Theodore Roosevelt.

Alice Roosevelt Longworth (1884-1980)

Longworth was the eldest child of U.S. President Theodore Roosevelt. Interested in politics, she married Nicholas Longworth (Republican-Ohio) who was the Speaker of the U.S. House of Representatives from 1925 to 1931. Their marriage was unconventional, and both parties had affairs. Alice's only child, Paulina, was sired from an affair with Senator William Borah of Idaho. Paulina died from an overdose in 1955, leaving Alice to raise her granddaughter. Known as a great wit, Alice is famous for saying, "If you haven't got anything nice to say about anybody, come sit next to me." She said of her father's need for attention, "My father always wanted to be the corpse at every funeral, the bride at every wedding, and the baby at every christening."

Calumet Farm (1924–)

Calumet Farm is a 762 acre farm in Lexington, Kentucky devoted to breeding and training Thoroughbred horses. Founded by William

Monroe Wright, owner of the Calumet Baking Powder Company, Calumet has the most recorded number of Kentucky Derby and Triple Crown winners and is considered the most famous Thoroughbred horse farm in the world. Calumet was handed down through the family until mismanagement ruined its legacy. It filed for bankruptcy in 1991 and family member, J. T. Lundy, was convicted of fraud and bribery in 2000. Calumet was later sold to an investment firm.

Dashiell Hammett (1894-1961)

Hammett is considered one of the greatest mystery writers of all time. He specialized in hard-boiled detective novels. His most famous works are *The Maltese Falcon* (Sam Spade novel), *The Thin Man* (Nick and Nora Charles), and *The Dain Curse*. He is associated with novelist and screenwriter, Lillian Hellman.

Eleanor Roosevelt (1884-1962)

Roosevelt served as First Lady of the United States from 1933 to 1945. During this time, Mrs. Roosevelt worked to expand the rights of working women, WWII refugees, and the civil rights of minorities. She advocated the U.S. join the United Nations and was appointed as its first delegate. Serving as first chair on the UN Commission on Human Rights, she oversaw the drafting of the Universal Declaration of Human Rights. Roosevelt later chaired President John Kennedy's Presidential Commission on the Status of Women. She was the niece of President Theodore Roosevelt and first cousin to Alice Roosevelt Longworth. Roosevelt married her fifth cousin once removed, Franklin Delano Roosevelt, who became the 32nd President of the U.S. She is considered one of the most admired people of the twentieth century.

Edward R. Bradley (1859-1946)

Edward Bradley was an American businessman and philanthropist. In 1906, he purchased Idle Hour Farm in Lexington, Kentucky. He exemplified the beginning wave of people with massive wealth buying land in the Bluegrass and pushing out the landed "aristocratic" families who had come to Kentucky between 1774 and 1830. A colorful character, Bradley identified himself as a speculator, raiser of racehorses, and a gambler. He won the Kentucky Derby in 1921, 1926, 1932, and 1933. He claimed that he was a friend of Wyatt Earp and knew Billy the Kid.

Flatfoot
Early 20th century slang for a police officer.

G-man
It is slang for an FBI agent.

George Raft (1901-1980)
Raft was an American movie star known for his gangster roles in the 1930s.

Git
Southerners pronounce "get" with a hard I when wanting to emphasize a warning. Get is often spelled git in Southern literature.

Great Depression (1929-1939)
The Great Depression was a world-wide phenomenon caused by the U.S. stock market crash in October 1929. The years 1931-1934 were the worst years of the Depression with an unemployment percentage rate of 15.9, 23.6, 24.9, 21.7 respectively, and even in 1940 unemployment was fifteen percent. President FDR's New Deal programs such as the CCC and the WPA helped

put the US back on its feet, but it wasn't until WWII that the country roared out of the Great Depression for good.

House of Saxe-Coburg and Gotha

A German dynasty founded by Ernest Anton, sixth duke of Saxe-Coburg-Saalfed. In Great Britain, the Saxe-Coburgs were descendants of (German) Albert, Prince Consort of (British) Queen Victoria (House of Hanover). In 1917, complaints about the British royal family's German surname caused King George V to change the name to the House of Windsor.

Isabel Dodge Sloane (1896-1962)

Isabel Dodge was an American heiress who won the 1934 Kentucky Derby with Cavalcade. Her father, John Dodge, co-founded the Dodge Brothers Motor Company. Her sister, Frances Dodge, also raced Thoroughbreds and owned Castleton Farm in Lexington, Kentucky.

James Cagney (1899-1986)

Cagney was an American actor, singer, and dancer, who is remembered for playing gangsters in *The Public Enemy*, *The Roaring Twenties*, and *White*

Heat. He won an Academy Award for his role in the musical *Yankee Doodle Dandy*. He is ranked eighth among American Film Institute's greatest male stars from the Golden Age of Hollywood. Orson Wells thought Cagney was "perhaps the greatest actor who ever appeared in front of a camera." Cagney is famous for smashing a grapefruit into Mae Clarke's face in *The Public Enemy*.

Jean Harlow (1911-1937)

Harlow was an American comedic actress and one of the first sex symbols of the "talkies." Known as the "Platinum Bombshell," she become one of Hollywood's biggest stars and is still ranked at No. 22 on AFI's greatest female stars of the Golden Age of Hollywood. Harlow died of kidney failure at the age of twenty-six.

Latonia Race Track

A Thoroughbred racing track in Covington, Kentucky, that opened in 1883 and was considered a major racing venue. It closed in 1939 due to the Great Depression, but reopened in 1959, having moved to Florence, Kentucky and renamed Turfway Park.

Longworth Family

A distinguished family from Cincinnati who made their money from wine. Nicholas Longworth I is remembered as the father of American wine making. Patrons of the arts, they donated land for parks and the Cincinnati Art Museum. Maria Longworth created the Rookwood Pottery Co. Nicholas Longworth III became Speaker of the House and married Alice Roosevelt. His campaigning for William Howard Taft on the Republican ticket for president, while Theodore Roosevelt also ran for president, caused an irreparable rift in his marriage to Alice.

Lucy Stone (1818-1893)

Lucy Stone was an American abolitionist and suffragist. She was the first woman from Massachusetts to earn a college degree in 1847. She is most remembered for using her maiden name after marriage. Women who use their maiden names rather than their husbands' surnames are called Lucy Stoners.

Mint Julep

A bourbon, sugar, mint, and shaved ice concoction served in a sterling cup. It is associated with the Kentucky Derby and Kentucky. Recipe–1 oz bourbon, 1 tsp of granulated sugar, and water. Pour into a silver cup with fresh mint leaves over shaved ice.

My Old Kentucky Home

Controversial song sung at the Kentucky Derby and is the official song of Kentucky. It was written by Stephen Foster as an anti-slavery song inspired by Harriet Beecher Stowe's *Uncle Tom's Cabin*. It describes a slave lamenting his being sold away from his Kentucky home. Frederick Douglass wrote in his 1855 autobiography, *My Bondage and My Freedom*, the song "awakens sympathies for the slave in which anti-slavery principles take root, grow, and flourish."

Parimutuel Betting

A system of gambling in sporting events when participants finished in a ranked order and the event is of short duration like horse racing. All bets are placed in a pool and shared among the winners. Illinois was the first state to introduce parimutuel betting to the U.S. in 1927. Laws regarding parimutuel betting differed from state to state.

Pennygate Farm

Imaginary horse farm for the purposes of this story.

Phoenix Hotel

An established landmark in Lexington, Kentucky, hailing from the 1820s, which catered to the well-to-do and those in horse racing. Generals from both the Union and Confederate armies used the Phoenix Hotel as headquarters during the American Civil War at separate times. In 1915, the Kentucky Equal Rights Association met there for a national suffragist meeting, and it was the site of Civil Rights protests during the 1960s. It was closed in 1977 and demolished in 1987.

Romeo y Julieta

A long cigar named after William Shakespeare's play—*Romeo and Juliet*. Established by Inocencio Alvarez and Manin Garcia in Cuba, 1875. It became nicknamed as the *Churchill* due to Winston Churchill's fondness for the cigar.

Seelbach Hotel

Historic hotel in Louisville, Kentucky founded by Louis and Otto Seelbach. It opened in 1905 as an ode to grand European hotels. F. Scott Fitzgerald used the Seelbach as inspiration for a hotel in *The Great Gatsby*.

Spats

Spats were a male fashion accessory, usually felt, that buttoned around the ankle and the arch of a shoe. They were intended to protect shoes from rain or mud. They fell out of use in the late 1920s.

Teddy Bears

A popular stuffed toy in the form of a bear. They were named after President Theodore "Teddy" Roosevelt and developed by Morris Michtom in the U.S. and Richard Steiff in Germany.

Theodore Roosevelt (1858-1919)

He was the 26th president (1901-1909) of the United States. He was known for saying "Walk softly and carry a big stick" which was based on an African proverb—"Walk softly and carry a big stick. You'll go far." This was the basis of Roosevelt's foreign policy to appear benign, but to use force if necessary when national interests are threatened. He is known as a conservationist and created the United States Forest Service, thereby establishing 150 national forests, 51 federal bird reserves, 4 national game preserves, and 5 national parks. During his presidency, Roosevelt protected 230 million acres of public land. In 1916, President Woodrow Wilson would continue Roosevelt's work by creating the National Park Service. As for his daughter, Alice Roosevelt Longworth, Roosevelt said, "I can be President of the United States or I can control Alice. I cannot possibly do both."

Wallis Simpson (1896-1986)

She was an American socialite, who began an affair with Edward David Windsor, Prince of Wales, and heir to the British throne in 1934. After her divorce from Ernest Simpson, Edward, now Edward VIII, King of Great Britain, created a constitutional crisis when he announced his intention to marry the twice-divorced Mrs. Simpson. He abdicated the throne in 1936 in order to marry her. Wallis Simpson is attributed with the quote, "You can never be too rich or too thin."

Wyatt Earp (1848-1929)

Iconic Old West lawman who is famous for the gunfight at the O.K. Corral in Tombstone, Arizona Territory, 1881. It is considered the most famous gunfight in the American West.

Other Books By Abigail Keam

Mona Moon Mysteries

Princess Maura Tales

Josiah Reynolds Mysteries

Last Chance For Love Series

About The Author

Hi. I'm Abigail Keam. I write the award-winning _Josiah Reynolds Mystery Series_. I also write the _Mona Moon 1930s Mystery Series_. Besides the _Josiah Reynolds_ and _Mona Moon Mysteries_, I write _The Princess Maura Tales_ (_Epic Fantasy_) and the _Last Chance For Love Series_ (_Sweet Romance_).

I am a professional beekeeper and have won awards for my honey from the Kentucky State Fair. I live in a metal house with my husband and various critters on a cliff overlooking the Kentucky River. I would love to hear from you, so please contact me.

Until we meet again, dear friend, happy reading!

9 781732 974395